Once Upon A Mountain

Bobbie Shafer

Publishers Note:
This is a work of fiction. All names, characters, places,
and events are the work of the author's imagination.
Any resemblance to real persons, places, or events is coin-
cidental.

Cover Art: Val Muller

Copyright ©Bobbie Shafer 2014
All rights reserved
ISBN 13: 978-0692235331
ISBN 10: 0692235337

Once Upon A Mountain   Bobbie Shafer

DWB PUBLISHING
www.dancingwithbearpublishing.com

~ One ~
A Trip to Say Goodbye

*L*ifting her head high, sniffing the air, the young doe detected a shift in the wind. Chirping ceased for a brief time and the bright eyes of the birds searched for a sign of danger. There was none. Sensing a change coming to the mountain, the animals and the birds were more curious than afraid.

For almost fifty years, the mountain remained the same—same people, same vegetation, same animals, and seasons came and seasons went as usual, but something different drifted in the air this day. The creatures were quiet and waited. But for what?

A sharp-eyed hawk, floating on the high currents above a clearing on the side of the mountain watched and waited. At the back of the clearing, nestled near a hill, sat a large cabin with soft yellow lights glowing through the windows. Nearby, a barn sheltered by a stand of pines, protected horses, a donkey, a cow and several seasonal visitors from the biting cold north wind. In the loft, a dozen or so woodland creatures created their winter homes by burrowing deep into the soft, sweet hay. In an attached shed, the chickens slept soundly in their safe refuge. The woodpile was stacked from the ground to the rooftop outside the north wall of the barn and the hen house kept out the bitter wind. The hens provided eggs all winter as long as they remained warm.

A large silvery-gray owl swooped out of the forest and landed on the snow-covered overhang of the loft. He wormed his way through a hole in the window into the uppermost region, hopped onto a support beam, shook and, preened his feathers, and rotated his head left and right. Seeing nothing, he shook himself and closed his eyes. The critters burrowed nervously deeper, froze, unmoving, except for their trembling but the tired old owl took no notice.

Inside the cabin, Letty Wade hummed softly, placed her bowl on a long, highly polished table, while a pot of oatmeal bub-bled on the wood stove. She reached for more bowls, shook her head, and turned around blinking in confusion, wondering why she thought she needed more bowls.

Smiling at the sound of soft muffled thumps from the porch roof, Letty glanced upward. The muted bumps alerted her to the local hawk heading into the attic for a rest, after having hunted all night.

"Hello, old boy," Letty murmured softly, "guess you're ready for a nap." Earlier that fall, when she saw the hawk around on the roof, eyeing the window, Letty removed several strips of wood from the ventilation window in the attic and replaced them with overlapping bands of leather.

Sighing, the woman piled a plate high with steaming biscuits and set a jar of homemade jam near her plate. With a long fork, she removed a large, sizzling slice of ham from the cast iron skillet and replaced the ham with two large eggs. The coffee sat near the back of the stove while Letty sipped on her third cup. The house was empty—too empty—so empty in fact that Letty often found herself talking to the many furry or feathered creatures that dropped by the cabin now and then. Today was no different.

"I guess you know, my fine feathered friend, you're nesting in the attic of one of the first cabins built on this mountain." Letty used her biscuit to sop up a mouth-watering bite of her over-easy, egg yolk. After swallowing, she looked upward again.

"I'll bet you didn't know my great-grandfather, Abner, built this place. My great-grandmother, Irene, and my grandmother and grandfather, Martha and Harmon, joined him soon after that." Another soft thump reached her ears. "I didn't think you knew." Letty smiled and spread some blackberry jam on her second biscuit.

"In fact, you're roosting over the very room they

built for Patience, Mama's sister, who came later after recovering from a broken leg". Letty paused when tears filled her eyes and she choked with emotion. "If your mother or grandmother flew around here back then, beautiful bird, they would remember that Patience was my best friend and everybody knew how close we were.

"Yes, dear hawk, great-grandfather, Abner, chose this place so his family could be near Kings Camp. The town had once been a site for the encampment for the soldiers of the English King George before America gained her freedom. Now it's a small town that serves the local settlers and   everyone here on the mountain."

Letty finished her breakfast while reminiscing and informing the disinterested hawk about the cabin. After swallowing the last bite, she rose, scraped all the leftovers in an old dented pan, and headed for the door. Outside, she divided the scraps into several containers scattered near the tree line. Turning, she looked over the back of the large, two-storied cabin.

Letty took a deep breath and sat on a nearby bench. "Dear hawk, I wish you had known my brothers. Mama and Pa named them Isaac and Elijah from the Bible. I came along a bit later. Mama named me Letitia after my late grandmother.

"It was Isaac that first called me *Letty*. Elijah just called me *Baby Girl*. They were the best brothers a girl could have. Those boys treated me like a princess, and as far as I was concerned, they could do no wrong. They were my heroes."

Letty rose and walked to the side of the cabin, looking across the valley at the silhouette of the mountains against the paling sky. Pulling her shawl around her, she tied it in front and entered the barn. While harnessing the horses, Pokey and Tiny to the wagon, Letty continued her trip down memory lane.

"You know, boys, old hawk up in the attic wasn't around when I was a girl, and neither were you two, now

9

that I think about it. I was only about ten years old when Isaac and Elijah decided to leave home, see the world, and search for a job up north. Mama and Papa were shocked when the boys announced their decision. I just refused to accept it. The day my brothers packed their clothes in their tattered traveling bags and walked down from the mountain, was the hardest day any of us ever faced. I was devastated.

"My mama used to tell me the story about the night I was born. That was the night Frank Wade announced he was gonna marry me." Letty paused and chuckled.

She fastened the final buckle on the harness and ran her hand down the side-strap along Pokey's side, up the horse's shoulder and rested her fingers on the halter. Leaning her cheek against Pokey's face, Letty inhaled deeply. The musky, salty smell of Pokey's coat brought a smile to her face. It was a comforting scent that only a country woman could appreciate. It was the smell of hard work, devotion, and dependability.

"I was telling you about the night I was born," she continued. "You would have loved Frank, Pokey. His parents, Daniel and Edwina, moved to the mountains a few years after the cabin was built. Mama and Pa became friends with the Wades and Mama and Edwina were there for each other during sickness, celebrations, canning season, and to assist in the births of all their babies.

"Frank was five when I arrived on the mountain, one cold December morning. When Edwina brought me out into the room for all to see, Mama said little Frank clapped his hands and said, 'I'm going to marry that baby someday.' Everybody laughed at him, but years later that remark became a fact."

Pokey snuffled and snorted. Letty laughed out loud. "Yes, he did, or at least that's what I was told. I dare say I don't remember it, but I've heard that story dozens of times." Giving the horse a final pat, Letty headed for the house to prepare for the trip ahead.

10

After cleaning up the kitchen, she washed and put away the dishes before climbing the stairs to her bedroom. Spreading the covers over her bed, she placed the carpet bag on the bed, and glanced at the old tintype picture a traveling photographer took of d Patience and her many years ago. Her eyes burned with tears. Taking the picture from the table, Letty pressed it against her breast and sat heavily in the old rocking chair. Her thoughts shifted back in time and memories flooded her mind.

"Oh, Patience," Letty murmured through her tears. "I can't believe you're gone. It seems like just yesterday we were happy-go-lucky young girls." Letty closed her eyes against the memories of days gone by.

~ * ~

Patience acted more like an older sister to Letty than she did an aunt. Being only ten years older than her niece, they shared a lot in common and later in years, Patience grew to love Frank like a brother. The girls spent all their time together, and when Patience fell in love with Henry Cobble, a boy from a nearby settlement, Letty missed the closeness she and Patience shared. However, when Patience's young man proposed and they moved to Seven Springs to start a new life, Letty was again devastated. Not only had she lost her brothers, but her best friend as well. Wade tried to comfort her and assure her that Patience's marriage wouldn't spoil their friendship and they would always be close.

Letty eventually relented and began to share in Patience's happiness. The day after Patience's marriage, when she and Henry drove away, Letty cried until dark. When she was cried out, she wrote Patience the first letter of many to follow. In fact, nearly fifty years' worth of letters traveled back and forth between the two friends. But Patience only returned to the mountains to attend her family members' funerals, and Letty's wedding to Wade.

Letty and Wade were together at every barn-raising,

11

during canning season, and attended all the church socials. The mountain folks watched them grow up, get closer, and it was no surprise when Wade showed up at Harmon and Martha's doorstep one spring evening asking for Letty's hand in marriage. At only fourteen, Letty loved Wade and although they both agreed to the marriage, Martha and Harmon insisted they wait to marry until the summer after Letty turned sixteen. The young couple reluctantly agreed to wait and the engagement announcement was made at the end of the church service the following Sunday.

Frank was one of five boys and with Letty's brothers gone, they both agreed it would be best to live with her parents so Martha and Harmon would have help with the chores and crops as they aged. Frank made plans to enlarge the cabin in order for everyone to have plenty of room.

When the wedding day arrived, Letty wore a lovely white dress hand-made by her mother. In a beautiful garden full of flowers and butterflies, Letty married Frank Wade. The family threw a grand party with fiddles, banjos, and harmonica music that had everyone jigging, clogging and two-stepping until the early morning hours.

Letty and Frank moved into the Walker cabin the next morning to begin their new life on the mountain. On the day following the wedding, knowing Letty's love for the mountain, Frank took her out to the garden.

"Sweet Letty," he said softly. "I've always known this was meant to be. I've been in love with you since the day you were born. When I look into your eyes, I see the love you have for this mountain. Every step I take in the woods, across the hills, and on the mountain trails, I feel your presence. This place is where the good Lord meant for you to be, and He meant for me to be by your side. I intend to make this cabin a castle for you and our family, and we'll live with our loved ones in peace and serenity."

"Oh, Frank," Letty said. "I love you so much. I'll

spend my life working by your side to create a proper king-dom for our castle."

True to his word, Frank spent the following year im-proving and adding onto to the cabin until it was the envy of the county. Along with Frank and Letty, her parents and grandparents, shared the spacious mountain home.

Shortly before their third anniversary, Frank and a neighbor went into the mountains to cut trees. There were always boards or planks that needed replacing. Repairing the walls, barns and fences was a full-time job, and the men wanted to make sure they had a good supply of fine lumber.

The rain started shortly after Frank left and when he wasn't back by late evening, Letty became worried. The next evening a search party located the two missing men at the bottom of a ravine. The downpour had caused flash floods and apparently the wagon had been swept off the mountain trail when the rain-soaked road collapsed under the weight of their wagon. Once again, Letty experienced a heartbreaking tragedy.

She buried her grandparents five years later. They passed within weeks of one another. Then, three years lat-er, her father died and her mother lasted only eight more months before joining him. Letty lived alone for nearly thirty-five years and her only regret was that she had never given Frank a child.

~ * ~

After the memories faded, Letty pushed herself from the rocking chair, replaced the photo on the table, grabbed her bag, and headed downstairs. She latched the front door securely and left by the rear door, twisting the key in the big padlock.

Pausing, she peered into the darkness, noticing the pans of food she put out earlier were not touched.

"You critters better eat up," she advised the gleaming eyes watching from the edge of the woods. "I'll be away a couple of days and there won't be snacks till I get back."

She swung her cloth bag around and trudged toward the barn where Pokey and Tiny, were restlessly waiting to take Letty to her destination. Leading the horses from the barn, she secured the door, climbed up on the wagon, threw her bag behind the wooden seat and flipped the reins. When the horses pulled the wagon out of the yard, Letty sighed. Pokey swung her head around and eyed her mistress. Letty was not using her normal happy voice and, apparently, the horses sensed her sadness.

With a heavy heart, Letty dreaded the thought of saying a final goodbye to Patience. She never failed to write her dear friend each month, and she would miss describing the beauty of the mountain and the daily activities of the area. She would also miss the anticipation of Patience's reply.

Letty couldn't remember the last time she had been away from home for more than a few hours, and that was just to run into Kings Camp for supplies four or five times a year. She welcomed the solitude of living miles from the nearest neighbor. The only roads from town went directly to someone's house and people on the mountain seldom had visitors, but lately she was feeling very, lonely.

Today she was heading to the Browning house to stay overnight with Patience's niece, Chastity, attend the funeral of her beloved aunt, and then head back to the comfort of her mountain. Once she was on the road, her thoughts wandered back to the dreams she had been having for the past few weeks.

Flicking the reins, Letty smiled at the way Pokey nodded, as if the horse understood her every movement. "Good girl, Pokey. I must say you're a pretty good listener. Don't know what I'd do without friend like you. Tiny is a good girl, too but not a very good talker, are you Tiny?"

Tiny didn't respond, but continued plodding down

the road.

"By the way, you two, I don't think I ever told you about those dreams I've been having. Now, I don't dream every night but at least two or three times a week. Lately, there are six tiny, beautiful flowers in a meadow but they're in danger of dying from a black cloud that surrounds them and kills all the other vegetation. The trees, grass, and the other vegetation around the flowers are brown and dead. However, the six flowers are huddling together for safety.

"You know, old girls, I've always had dreams like Grammy had—dreams that announced birth, drought, flood, or even death, but this dream is disturbing and confusing. I don't know anyone about to have a baby, the weather is pleasant, scattered showers are regular, and I don'tt feel any danger."

Pokey snorted and nodded again. Tiny shook her head. Letty continued, "I thought when I got the notice that Patience was gone, the dream would stop butt didn't. I wonder what the number six means, and why flowers? It surely is a puzzle and I wish the dreams would stop."

Pokey didn't answer this time and Letty smiled at her foolish attempt to hold a conversation with a horse. Shaking her head, she urged them on.

When they passed through Kings Camp an hour or two before lunch, Letty rested the horses and munched on a couple of slices of bread and a piece of dried beef. Late that evening, just before dark, Letty stopped the wagon along the sidewalk in front of Cornelius and Chastity Browning's house. A servant ran out to take the reins while another helped her down and carried her beat-up suitcase into the house.

"Oh, Aunt Letty," a young woman gushed, pecked Letty on both cheeks, barely grazing her skin. "I'm so glad you're finally here. Let me show you upstairs where you can freshen up. We're having a light supper in the dining

room in half an hour. I'll send the maid to fetch you."
The house buzzed with muted chatter from Chastity's family and friends, who were strangers to Letty.

She washed her hands and face, and made up her mind she wouldn't unpack. She took a deep breath before returning downstairs and facing all of those unknown people.

Although Chastity called her *Aunt*, they weren't truly related and knew Chastity didn't actually consider her family. Letty planned to leave from the cemetery to start back home. At least she was honest with herself. All the sparkle and glitter designed to advertise their wealth made her uncomfortable and she wanted to go home. A country girl was always a country girl.

The crystal candelabras on the tables, and the immense chandelier hanging above the table, glittered brightly and made Letty's eyes water to look at them for very long. The plates were of the finest china and water filled the most delicate imported crystal goblets. She shook her head and thought of her dear Aunt Patience living amid all this gaudy display, among these pompous people. Patience was the most down-to earth person she knew and had no tolerance for waste or expensive living. Patience believed that man was meant to work hard, live simply, love deeply, and honor the Lord. Letty felt living here must have been difficult for Patience.

Letty retired to her room immediately after dinner, pulled off her shoes, which pinched her toes. Shrugging out of her confining jacket, Letty unbuttoned the top button of her high-necked blouse, and exhaled in relief. Carefully folding her traveling clothes, she placed them on the chest of drawers, slipped into her gown and robe. She dozed off sitting in a chair by the bedroom window. Exhausted from the trip and the emotions of saying farewell to a beloved aunt devoured her energy.

She stood on a hill looking toward a meadow. Six lovely flowers bent by a strong wind caused them to nearly touch the ground. They wrapped their leaves around each other to keep from snapping off at their stems. The force of the wind made them tremble, yet they protected one another and stood firm. A hawk sat on a nearby limb and cried, "Help them, Letty. Give them some hope." She glanced at the bird, and when she looked back at the flowers, they were weeping. The wind suddenly changed direction and buffeted her face, stinging her skin with a freezing bite.

Letty gasped and jerked awake.

Closing the bedroom window, Letty straightened the wind-blown curtain and brushed the light layer of snow from the window sill. She shrugged out of her robe and slid into bed. She couldn't wait to get home. This wasn't her kind of life, and wanted to be back on the mountain. She needed the peace and quiet of her home, and she also needed time to solve the mystery of the dream.

By the next morning, the weather had taken a turn for the worse. The sky darkened and sleet joined the falling snow. The funeral was bleak and dismal. The wind whipped through clothing like a sharp knife. Umbrellas were ripped inside out, and hats were sent flying. Icy pellets stung the mourners' faces, and most of them turned their backs to protect their exposed skin from the onslaught of ice and snow. The dreariness of the weather added to the pain and sadness Letty felt.

Her heart grew heavier every minute. She knew she would never be able to drive through this storm. The struggle through the cold and piling snow would be disastrous for the horses. Tiny was young and tough, but Pokey was beginning to feel his age and probably wouldn't be able to make it to Kings Camp before his joints stiffened. It just wouldn't be fair to the horses. They had been with Letty for most of their lives and she would make sure they were cared for.

The coffin slowly sank into the grave and the mourners dropped the few flowers they had been able to find. Chastity sniffed dramatically and Cornelius patted her back and handed her his handkerchief. Letty bit her lip to stifle sobs that threatened and slowly made her way back to the waiting carriages.

Once they were back at Chasity's house, Letty felt even more depressed to find that not only was most of Chastity's family there, but so were a couple of dozen neighbors and friends. More than likely, these people only saw Patience once or twice, and had dropped in to hear the latest gossip. Feeling guilty for being so anti-social and judgmental, Letty couldn't help but wonder if they were being respectful or just nosey. She found an empty chair in the corner and tried to become invisible.

Several ladies standing near the punchbowl chatted about what a shame it was that such a dreadful place operated right under everyone's nose. It was a lucky thing, they whispered, that the authorities found out before another child was injured or died.

Letty almost jumped out of her chair when they mention a child being hurt or killed. She contemplated joining them but paused when a younger woman joined them near the end of the conversation.

"What place are you talking about?" the young woman asked. "That orphanage they just closed several weeks ago?"

The heavy-set woman who had been talking earlier, leaned forward and whispered hoarsely, "Yes, there had been some suspicion of embezzlement, and when they investigated, it was discovered the children were being worked from dawn to dark. They were barely being fed enough to keep them alive, and were freezing to death. Also, the administrator was pocketing all the donations and state funds.

"Oh, yes, *she* had a warm suite of rooms, ate roast chicken and steak, but those poor children ate some kind of tasteless mush three times a day. The board discovered the children had only one thin blanket each and half of them were sick." The woman hesitated, looked over her shoulder and continued, "I heard a rumor that several had starved to death, or died from lack of medical treatment."

A nearby woman gasped. "Can you imagine such cruelty?"

The women shook their heads, dabbed their eyes, and one muttered, "Oh my, no, I can't. How could she have gotten away with it for so long without being discovered? And what in the world is the state doing about it?"

The heavily corseted woman cleared her throat, looked around again, and when her friends leaned forward, she lowered her voice. "I know there's about a dozen in the hospital. Many were transferred to other orphanages, some were put on the orphan train heading west to find homes for them out there, and some were adopted by families in nearby counties." She paused and patted her fancy hair-do.

"What about the ones in the hospital?" her friend asked. "I'd hate to think of them running around town spreading disease or sickness, or whatever it is they have."

"I believe they're all spoken for," the woman assured her. "The doctors said they were just undernourished and dehydrated, or something along that line. They had scurvy from not getting vitamin C or D or one of those letters. But once they started getting the correct food, they began to recover. They located all of them to safe places, except for five or six, or so I heard. If they can't find a place for them, I hear they'll be sent to the work house. I guess that's better than begging in the streets, especially at this time of year. I hate to think of them cluttering up the street corners. That's so unseemly and really down-grades a neighborhood."

"I wish we could take them in, but with my delicate nerves and poor Duncan working three and four days a week at his father's shipping office, it just wouldn't be fair to the sweet children," piped up the newcomer. "Plus, I just can't abide hiring a governess and having another stranger in the house. I even sent my own dear children off to boarding school as soon as the school would take them so that poor, overworked Duncan could get some rest and my nerves wouldn't be strained."

"Pardon me," Letty said, clearing her throat. "How many children did you say might be placed in the work-house?"

The women turned slowly and looked Letty up and down, not just once but twice. One or two of the women looked up toward the ceiling and shook their heads, while another lifted her scented handkerchief to her nose and sniffed loudly.

"I beg your pardon?" The plump lady fanned her face. "Are you addressing me? Do you work here? I don't believe I've seen you around before."

Letty glared at the woman. "No, madam, I don't work here. My name is Letty Wade and I am Patience's niece. I asked you how many children did not find a home."

"I didn't know my close friend, dear, dear, Patience, had a niece."

The fat lady's friend smiled and sniffed haughtily. "I don't recall her or Chastity ever mentioning you before. You don't live around here, do you?"

"You know, I'll bet there are a great many things you don't know, ma'am, but I do know that you were not one of my aunt's closest friends. If you were, you'd know who I am. Patience was more than just my aunt, we were friends, best of friends—dearest of friends. And if you were close friends, you'd know that, just like I'd know about you. Believe me, I am as relieved as you are that we are not acquainted.

"Now, back to my question. How many children in the orphanage did not find a home? You seem to know everything else that goes on around here, and the orphanage apparently. Do you know the exact number of children left?"

The woman was struck dumb by Letty's forwardness, nerve, and irritated tone. Her friend answered for her. "I b-believe she said five or six, didn't you, Viola? I don't think she's exactly sure how many, are you, Viola dear?"

Viola shook her head quickly and stepped back.

"Thank you and good day," Letty snapped and turned around. She marched upstairs, quickly packed her small, ragged case, bundled up in her coat, snugged her hat down on her head, and headed downstairs to thank Chastity for her hospitality. She marched up to her hostess, kissed her cheek, stiffened, and looked around the room.

"I can't tell you how much I appreciate your letting me stay here for the funeral, dear, but I recently discovered some things I need to see about." Letty spoke softly and chose her words carefully.

"But Miss Letty, you just can't go out in this weather, it's terrible out there. Please, let me have someone take your suitcase back to your room. You simply must stay, at least until the storm is over. I know you are anxious to get home but be reasonable."

Chastity was horrified that Letty was leaving. What would the neighbors say about her guest leaving in such a storm? They would wonder, and no doubt, gossip over the reason for Letty's hasty departure. Chastity followed Letty to the door.

"Miss Letty, I don't know why you insist on leaving now, but there is a storm coming and it isn't safe. You simply must stay until the weather clears," Chastity whispered. "I can't be responsible for your safety if you leave now. What will people think?" Chastity gripped Letty's el-

21

bow tightly.

Letty frowned, pulled away from Chastity's grip, and opened the door. Suddenly, a tall, older gentleman touched her arm.

"Excuse me, madam, but are you Letty Wade, Miss Patience's niece? The Miss Letty that lives on the mountain?"

"Y-e-s." Letty narrowed her eyes suspiciously.

"Forgive me, my name is Franklin McDougan. I was your Aunt Patience's lawyer and I must plead with you to stay over until tomorrow for the reading of the will. There are a few things that Miss Patience wanted you to have. It was very important to her that you be here to receive her gift."

"What time is the reading?" Letty asked sharply.

"Three o'clock on the dot, and I promise we won't waste one second," Franklin assured her.

"Very well, I'll return at that time. I'm going to check into the nearest hotel. I have some things I need to take care of. I'll see you tomorrow at three, no later, mind you. If you're not prepared by then, you can contact me by mail," Letty said firmly.

Chastity elbowed past Franklin and clasped her hands. "Hotel? Miss Letty, no, please, we have plenty of room here. What happened to change your mind? I thought you were staying until after the storm." Chastity looked around to see if anyone was eavesdropping.

"Chastity, honey, this is not my world and I cannot stay here. I thank you for your hospitality but I don't feel comfortable here. I do not believe in wasting whatever precious time I have left in a place I do not belong. Hotels are for strangers passing through, or visiting a place for a short time, and that's what I am here in Seven Springs. I am a stranger.

"Please, do not concern yourself. I came here to say goodbye to Patience and I have done that. I'm not going to travel in this weather, so you're not to worry. Goodbye, my dear. I hope you have a good and comfortable life."

"Miss Letty, this is ridiculous. Why spend hard earned money on a hotel when..." She saw the grim, determined look on Letty's face and sighed. "At least let me have someone drive you." Chastity's plea was to empty air. Letty was out the door and down the steps.

Stunned, Chastity recalled her husband telling her about the stories he heard of the people living in the mountains. They were rumored to be odd, ignorant, and superstitious clods. In the beginning, he had been against Patience moving in with them until he overheard a conversation at a poker game that quickly changed his mind. He promised his wife she wouldn't be sorry allowing Patience to spend her final days with them. They both agreed they would not allow Patience to associate with their friends, and both avoided the woman as much as possible. That inconvenience was over now that she was finally gone. But this woman, another mountain woman, was here and being difficult. Would this aggravation never end?

"Should I send Cornelius after her?" She wrung her hands together.

"Don't worry Miss Chastity, I'll drive her and make sure she's safe," Mr. McDougan quickly assured her. "My carriage is just down the street."

Chastity hurried away while Franklin waited for the maid to bring his coat.

"I have something to tell Miss Letty that is going to change her life. I have a feeling that this woman deserves the kind of change that's coming her way, and I'm glad to be the one to deliver the news," he muttered and smiled when he saw the maid scurrying toward him.

~ Two ~
Ask Me No Questions

*F*ranklin McDougan grinned, jerked on his coat, jammed his hat on tightly, pulled his collar up around his ears, and raced after Letty, who was marching steadily down the sidewalk.

"Miss Letty," he called. "My carriage is right here. Allow me to drive you to the proper hotel. I know one where you will be safe and comfortable."

"Mister McDougan, you must know that I have limited funds. All I need is a warm room, a comfortable bed, and a cup of tea or coffee. Something plain and simple will do just fine."

"I understand, Miss Letty. I know just the place. Please, let me help you with your bag."

"Thank you, sir. I truly do appreciate your kindness. Perhaps, you could assist me with something else. You see, I just found out that there are—"

"My time is yours, Miss Letty, but please, let's get in the carriage and out of this cold wind. My hands are numb, my ears are cold, and I can't feel my nose. In other words, dear lady, I'm freezing."

"Oh, forgive me, Mister McDougan. I guess I'm just a tough old mountain woman used to being out in this kind of weather. The livestock and chickens have to be fed and watered regardless of how low the temperature gets."

Inside the carriage, they proceeded down the snow covered street and Letty asked Franklin about the orphanage and received almost the same story she had heard the women recite. There were, as the woman had said, five or six children waiting. Tomorrow was the final day to relocate. The movers would be there to strip the building and prepare it for dismantling. Whatever children remained would be sent to the workhouse. Franklin assured her that the workhouse provided good food and warm rooms.

"Mister McDougan, ask me no questions for I have no answers but I must have those children. I don't have any money to pay you but next summer when I sell my jellies and jams at the town fair, I will send you every dime I earn. Will you help me get those children? You have my word that I will pay whatever you charge, maybe not all at once but eventually, you will get your money."

"Miss Letty, I do not doubt for a second that you pay your debts and it would be my honor to represent you in obtaining those children. In fact, if you hand me a copper penny, I will, in all legal rights, become your retained attorney. I assure you that you will have no problems.

"I don't think the state wants to send children to the workhouse but every other place is filled to capacity, even the orphan train was full. Believe me, I know they checked everywhere."

"I just thought that, well, I'm almost fifty-nine and I live up in the mountains. I know what they say about mountain folks. They think we're all backward, uneducated, and our children run around unwashed and dirty. I'm afraid they just might think that I'm—"

"I assure you, as Patience's attorney, I will attest to your excellent qualifications and will be honored to speak on your behalf. I know for a fact that those stories concerning residents of the mountains are farfetched and ridiculous. You'd be surprised at the friends your Aunt Patience had. I imagine that most of the *Members of the Board of Children's Assistance* knew your aunt personally, and know those wild tales of mountain people are nonsense As I said, I don't think you'll have any problems. I just wonder why would you—?"

"No questions, please. I said before, I have no answers you would understand. I don't understand them myself," Letty said wearily. "But I know, or rather, I *feel* I'm supposed to do this."

"Please, call me Franklin. May I call you Letty?" When Letty nodded, he continued. "Your aunt spoke of you so often I feel I know you personally, and I hope you don't mind my telling you this, but she used to read me parts of your letters each month. Those letters were her pride and joy. She looked forward to them regularly and never failed to tell me when she received one. I feel I know the store-keeper, that Indian trapper friend of yours, and a few of your neighbors. Especially that lady, Mrs. Slocum, who can clod dance the quills off a porcupine and the stink off a skunk."

Letty burst into laughter while tears formed in her eyes. "I had no idea they meant much so much to her. I would have written more often except not much happens on the mountains. I should have described each day for her as her old home was her greatest pleasure. I loved hearing from her, too, but her letters just made me glad I lived where I did and wished she was with me. She and my mother were not only sisters but best friends.

"She was like an older sister to me and I mourned her moving away just as painfully as I mourn her passing. She was the last connection to my past. All of my family is gone now. My brothers left for the north to find work when I was young. I haven't seen them since the day they walked down the mountain.

"I bet Aunt Patience asked me a dozen times if I'd ever heard from them. She never gave up the idea that someday they'd return. I even got to believing they might come home someday because of her. Of course, it would be a miracle this late in the game. How did you meet Aunt Patience?"

Franklin chucked at the memory of that meeting. "I started to say you wouldn't believe it but knowing her as well as you do, you probably will.

"I had gone to lunch at my club, which is a private men's club, I might add. Apparently, she went to my office and when my secretary told her where I was, she just marched right in and demanded that I be told she was there. The gentleman in charge tried to explain that ladies weren't allowed to enter the club, but she wouldn't take that as an acceptable answer.

"He immediately summoned me and how glad I am that she insisted. She was a gem in the crown of my life. That woman told me stories of her life in the mountains, her family, especially all about you, her marriage to the love of her life, even though his dreaming and gambling kept them in the poorhouse. She loved him till the very end and—well, that's another story.

"Although she was your aunt, after a while, I began to feel a bond growing between Patience and me, and she became a part of my family, too. I looked forward to our meetings, and sometimes dropped by to see her for no rea-son other than to spend time with her. I never tired of hearing her tell me about life on the mountain.

"Oh, here we are at the hotel I was talking about. You just hurry in out of the cold. I'll make sure you have your bag and see that it's brought in."

Letty thanked Franklin and stepped down from the carriage before anyone could help her. Then she rushed in-to the warm, cozy lobby of the small hotel.

Franklin came in directly behind her, along with his driver, Joseph, carrying Letty's suitcase.

"Mister McDougan, what a pleasant surprise to see you. Don't tell me you need a room." A young man with a wide infectious grin and twinkling eyes stood before them.

"No, Mister Porter, I don't need a room. I have brought you a customer, however. Someone I think you'll be more than happy to meet.

"May I introduce Mrs. Letty Wade from near Kings Camp? She is Miss Patience's niece come for the funeral. She would like one of you nicest rooms with a hot bath, please."

"Mister McDougan, I thought you understood—" Cut off when Robert Porter reached out and began to vigorously shake her hand, Letty smiled.

"Mrs. Wade, how do you do? What a pleasure to

27

meet the niece of Miss Patience. Did Mister McDougan tell you if it wasn't for that dear lady I wouldn't have this hotel?"

When Letty shook her head, Porter continued. "My father, Robert Senior, was a doorman at a big hotel in St. Louis. I was a boy in those days. He loved that old hotel and talked for many years about having one of his own. I swore to myself that I would someday try to make his dream come true. I went to work at that same old hotel in St. Louis and worked in every department they had. When my father retired we came here and I tried everywhere to get a loan on our combined experience, but to no avail. Experience is no substitute for collateral.

"Mister McDougan was in the bank one day when I applied for a loan and when I left, he followed me and told me to call upon him later in the week. When I did, I met your aunt and she wrote me a letter and vouched to financially back me in obtaining that loan. The bank didn't hesitate. We bought this old building, renovated it, and my father and I now have a comfortable little income. My father's dream is realized—thanks to your aunt. That woman is, oh, forgive me, was a saint."

Letty looked astounded. She never dreamed her aunt had so much influence in business matters. "I'm so pleased that my aunt was able to help you and your father. That's the kind of person she was, but I'm afraid that I cannot afford—"

"Mrs. Wade, if you think for one moment that I would charge for the pleasure of having you stay in my hotel, you are greatly mistaken. You and your family have a room here at no cost to you for as long, and as often, as you would like to stay. It is entirely my pleasure and I simply won't take *no* for an answer." With that, he snapped his fingers, summoning a young boy who snatched up Letty's carpet bag.

"Madam Wade, this is my son, Andrew. Andrew, this is Mrs. Letty Wade, a very important person. I want you to take this fine lady's luggage to room ten, please, the one in the back, on the corner. Make sure the fire is lit and have one of the girls fill the tub with hot water and provide plenty of towels and fresh linen.

"Miss Letty, I will have our complimentary lunch sent to your room as soon as you're refreshed. I am so honored by your presence. Please, let me offer my condolences on the loss of your aunt and my dear benefactor. The world has lost a generous woman, a dear friend, and your loving aunt. It was a much, much better place with her among us."

Letty was at a loss for words. She stared at Robert Porter Jr., his son, Andrew, and lastly, at Franklin McDougan, who stood smiling slyly.

"I, uh, I thank you, Mister Porter for your kindness and your generosity. I appreciate the room and I'm sure my aunt received great joy from assisting you."

~ * ~

A change was coming and it had begun. Back on the mountain, the hawk soared and screeched a cry that echoed across the mountainside and caused the foxes and mice to scatter. The deer stiffened, raised their heads and carefully surveyed the meadow and foothills. The wind picked up speed and swept down into the valleys, scattering thistles in the air like a celebration of nature.

The birds chattered nosily and the wolves called mournfully to one another across the hilltops. In the barn, the owl swayed, opened his sleepy eyes, hooted a haunting cry, and returned to his slumber. All living creatures on the mountains sensed that something was about to change but they were confused. The air was clean, the sky was clear, and there were no strange sounds to warn them of danger. Whatever was happening did not cause them alarm. It was more like curiosity. Like a sound they couldn't identify, a smell that seemed to calm them, to reassure them. They returned to normal, at least until they had reason again to listen.

The wind picked up that comforting scent, that smell, lifting it high, above the clouds, and pushed it north and eastward, scattering it among all the towns to remind people of their beginnings--of their childhood and their homes. A few people raised their heads, sniffed, smiled, and walked on, remembering things of long ago. The scent drifted southward, touching people wherever it went, warming their hearts, and lifting their spirits.

~ * ~

The gigantic cold, gray, lifeless building had been filled with misery and torment since the day it was built. The original sign now faded, still faintly visible, read "Imports" but that was just a ploy to disguise the slaves brought here before being sent to the auction block. That was years ago but during that time, frightened men, women, and children terrified of being separated from their family, some alone and sick, were forced to lay shackled to the floor. When the slavery debates began, rumors of war started, brother turned against brother, and the building was abandoned and eventually sold. A greedy businessman worked women and children up to sixteen hours a day in his manufacturing plant, sewing uniforms and blankets for the army during the war. After Lee surrendered and the war was finally over, the factory became a refuge to house wounded and sick soldiers, and later, a convalescent home for those who needed long term care.

Due to the scarcity of medical supplies, their recovery was long and painful. When the surviving soldiers returned home, left to start life over, and the less fortunate were laid to rest, the building was sold again. The owners leased the structure to the state to use as a home for the homeless and orphaned children of the state.

Those who knew of the building's history hoped that, at last, it would be used for a good cause. Religious leaders turned in names of children who had lost their parents, and the policemen who patrolled the streets, knew first-hand of all the homeless children running wild stealing to eat, made homes in abandoned buildings, and caused the local residents to worry about having their pockets picked.

The administrators of the orphanage were delighted to take in as many children as they could cram into the rooms, since the state paid a handsome sum for each child under their care. Little did the state and locals know that all the money went into the pockets of the headmistress and her personal staff.

Many inspectors also benefited from money slipped to them for an appropriate report. Purchases of quality food were rare and the finest food was allotted for the staff. Large sacks of cereal, rejected potatoes and crates of molded cabbage were acquired for the children. Bread was rare and meat was hardly ever seen except when the members of the board dropped by for the bi-annual inspections.

Most of the employees realized quickly that their cooperation with the matron and upper staff was rewarded, while those who complained about the conditions of the children, lack of heat, and poor quality of food were either fired or given the hardest jobs and never promoted. Cooperation was rewarded with raises. The majority who complained either quit or was eventually driven out.

Daisy Epperson and one or two others were exceptions to the rule. They were warm and loving people whose concern for the children was more important than money or position. They stayed since they felt the children needed someone who cared, someone who would be there for them.

Finally, after losing so many to pneumonia, fevers, and sickness due to lack of proper food, Daisy sent letters to one or two members of the board she had met and felt were genuinely concerned about the welfare of the orphans.

An investigation ensued, surprise visits were arranged, and an accountant from the state uncovered state monies were being embezzled. Conclusions were made to shut down the orphanage and relocate all the children.

Daisy Epperson's snappy footsteps echoed loudly throughout the empty space of the four-storied building that once housed over one hundred cold, hungry orphans. The movers loaded all the furniture, except Daisy's and returned to the cold, bare building to remove the kitchen stove and Daisy's bed, the only furniture left.

She opened her bedroom door and saw the six remaining children huddled together for warmth on a quilt in the corner. Only her room contained wood for the fireplace. Although it wasn't warm enough by any means, at least it wasn't freezing as were the other rooms. The glass panes were frosted inside and a chill filled the room. Foggy breath hung in the air when they exhaled or spoke.

"Come, children, it's time to go," Daisy said softly. She volunteered to remain after all the staff had been dismissed. The state relocated many of the children, while Daisy and two members of the state committee searched to find places for some. Once the decision to shut down had been made, Daisy and two others had been found innocent of any wrong doing, and she alone volunteered to stay and care for the remaining children until they left for the work house.

She begged everyone she knew to take the last six children in, but everyone had large families and others weren't financially able. Times were hard except for the very wealthy, and they couldn't be bothered.

Delbert Manheim, director of the workhouse, was a kind man who assured her that he would find a position for each child and would take good care of them. He explained that although the children were forced to work, they also were provided with three meals a day. It was the last place she wanted them to go, but it was the only place that would accept them. It was also their last hope.

One of the street vendors delivered seven sausage and egg pies, while someone else sent a pot of hot chocolate for the children's last morning.

~ * ~

"Put your coats on and go near the fire. We've been given some delicious pies and hot cocoa for breakfast and then we must get ready to leave," Daisy said sadly. "I'll get the food."

She watched them stiffly rise and Chloe, the twelve year old, began to help the other girls, Eveline and Grace, who were ten and six, button their thin coats. Daniel, eleven, was in the corner and as he climbed over Eli and Oliver, eight year old twins, he shivered and grabbed his jacket.

"Pies? W-what kind did you s-say, Miss Daisy?" Oliver's teeth chattered and he scrambled to uncover himself with his coat and put it on. His hands were so cold that he had trouble buttoning up, especially since the buttons were different sizes and were hard to cram through the buttonholes.

Daisy moved near the fire and opened a metal bucket, "I think Mister Willowby said the pies were sausage and eggs. Mrs. Brazzi sent her famous hot cocoa. They were so kind. Aren't we lucky?"

"I'll say," Eli said. "My stomach thinks my mouth has been sewed shut, it's been so long since I've eaten."

"You're always hungry," his twin, Oliver said teasingly.

The eerie silence of the empty house was suddenly broken by loud banging on the door.

"Are they coming for us already?" Eveline asked tearfully. "Can't we stay with you, Miss Daisy, can't we?"

"I wish you could, my darlings, but I got a housekeeping job and I'll be working six days a week. I put in my application for custody of all of you, but they didn't think I'm qualified to care for six children under twelve. I'm only seventeen and they didn't approve me 'cause I don't make enough money, and I live in the servant's quarter where I work. Please believe me, my little ones, I did try."

"It sounds better than the workhouse," Daniel grumbled.

"That may be true but it ain't up to me," Daisy said sadly. "You know I'd take you if there was any possible way."

The pounding became louder and more insistent.

"You go on and eat. I'll see who's at the door. I'll keep 'em busy until you've finished. Maybe it's just some more movers or someone to see the building," she said hopefully.

They listened to her footsteps clicking on the tile floor and when it faded away, they began to gobble the pies and sip the cocoa as fast as they could, all the while, listening.

When Daisy didn't return after a few minutes, Chloe tiptoed to the door and opened it a crack. She listened intently and the rest waited expectantly for a report. She turned, shook her head and shrugged. "I don't hear a thing," she said. "Not a sound."

"What if she went off to her new job and left us all alone," Grace said and sniffed. "I'm scared. What if—?"

"Hush," Chloe snapped. "Daisy wouldn't do that. She stayed behind to care of us. She's coming back. I'm sure of it. Let's be patient and finish our breakfast."

However, Chloe wasn't confident Daisy would return, and felt that Grace could be right. They had been starved, cold, and alone for so long that it was nearly impossible to completely trust anyone. The only people they truly trusted were each other. Regardless of the consequences, they would stay together. If anyone, anyone at all, tried to separate them, she and Daniel had already decided that they would run away and survive somehow. It couldn't be any harder than working from dawn to dark, going hungry, and sleeping on a rock hard, weed filled mattress like they had at the orphanage. She and Daniel could manage. They had to.

They finished their pies and when the last drop of hot chocolate was gone, they sat silent, alone, and very

34

afraid. It seemed like Daisy had been gone for hours.

When the door finally opened, Daisy came in slowly, tears streaming down her cheeks. Chloe pulled Eveline and Grace close to her and the twins snuggled up behind Daniel.

Daniel reached out and took Chloe's hand. Whatever hardship they had to face, he would make sure none of them faced it alone—after all, they still had each other. "It's all right. We're together."

"D-Daisy?" Grace asked with trembling lips. "Is it time? Have they come for us? Is the workhouse man here?" Daisy pulled up her apron, covered her face, and gave two heavy sobs. "Daisy? What's wrong? Won't they take us? Oh, Daisy, please tell us what's wrong?" Chloe cried miserably.

"N-n-nothing's wrong, my dearies, nothing. That's just it. These are not tears of sadness but of joy." She smiled and wiped her wet face. She grabbed Grace and held her close.

"Joy?" Daniel asked incredulously. "Joy? Daisy, who was at the door? What is so joyous? Have you gone mad?"

"Sit down, children and listen well. Eveline, do you remember that dream you told me about? You know, the one where you and the others were in a field, and darkness and desolation was creeping in all around you. You said there was a hawk flying overhead calling to you not to be afraid, that help was on its way. Don't you remember?"

Daisy saw Eveline nod but knew that her creased forehead was a sign of worry. The child's lips were trembling and tears gathered in her brown eyes.

"The hawk was right, Evie, the hawk was right. A lady just came by this morning with a lawyer man who contacted the state committee, drew up the proper papers, signed them, and has come to take you home with her. She's adopted you."

"No," Eveline screamed. "No, I won't go. I don't want to go. I want to stay with the others. Please don't take me away. Why can't we all stay together? Please, please."

"Don't take Eveline away, please, Miss Daisy. We have to stay together, we just have to. You understand don't you? Help us, please." Grace cried, while tears cascaded down her cold-reddened cheeks. She grabbed Eveline around the waist and hugged her tightly. "Don't take her away."

Daniel slumped and squeezed Chloe's hand as she gasped at the news, his bravery slipping away. "You don't understand. I'm so sorry, children. It's not just Eveline. It's all of you. Everyone. Chloe, Eveline, Grace, Daniel, Eli and Oliver. All of you." Daisy sobbed even harder seeing their faces fill with doubt and suspicion. They all grabbed hands and held tight to one another.

"Now, she's not as young as me, but she looks gentle and kind. She says she lives on a mountain that is covered in trees, flowers, little creatures that eat from your hand, and the sky is the bluest in the land, and filled with songbirds, owls and clouds of the softest white you ever saw. Children, I think you're the luckiest of them all. I'll bet none of the others are going to a better place than you are. I would just love to live on a mountain."

She nearly laughed and the children could see she truly believed what she was saying.

Chloe took the girls' hands and began to dance around. "Come, Daniel, grab a hand and join in," she shouted, even though Daniel didn't look totally convinced.

"No time to dance, Chloe," Daisy said. "They're waiting for you all this very minute. She says the snow's stopped and if you all leave right now, you won't get cold and wet. Get up and button your coats. Take your blankets. I think she just has a wagon and it might be cold on the trip." The children buttoned their coats tightly and wrapped their blankets around them like shawls. Nervously they glanced at one another and gave each other a weak smile. They walked toward the door and each stopped to give Daisy a long hug. It was a tearful goodbye, but Daisy's tears were mostly for the joy of their rescue from the workhouse. Any place was better than that and she had a good feeling they were headed for a good place, a place every child should be. Home. She gave a thankful prayer, looked around at the cold, bare room, and closed the door.

The trip down the stairs felt like an eternity. Chloe held her sisters' hands tightly and felt their fear, their loneliness, and their uncertainty as they went to meet the woman who would take them away, and to what?

Daniel, who was always suspicious, also held the hands of the twins, who were delighted to go anywhere other than the workhouse. He tugged them along. He was determined to save them, even if it was from themselves.

Letty heard the children coming down the stairs and stepped from the office, where they signed the legal papers, to see the six children she had just adopted, sight unseen. Although she knew their ages, she was unprepared to see six children so small, so fragile, and so frightened. Her feeling of surprise turned quickly to anger. Anger at how the world could abandon its children. There was a time, not so long ago, when she had been taught that it took a village to raise a child. Her grandmother told her when she was small, caring for a child was everyone's job, and each neighbor watched out for everyone else's child. They fed them when they were hungry, took them in when there was illness or tragedy, and never, never did anyone wonder if their children would be taken care of if they were alone, for they were never alone. Now, in this big city, no one seemed to care if children begged in the streets, if they went hungry or were cold. They just didn't seem to care at all. Here were six examples of that standing right before her. How could children like this be neglected?

Franklin appeared at her elbow and whispered, "Miss

Letty, I think you'd better say something. The children look a little frightened. I don't think they know what's happening to them. This is an unexpected, last minute reprieve and they seem to be quite uncertain of the situation. Maybe you can ease their fear."

Letty blinked back to the present and smiled at the six curious faces. "Hello, my name is Letty Wade and I've come to take you home. I thought we could leave this morning but Mister McDougan says we must wait until later. I have to attend the reading of a will this afternoon, but we'll leave as soon as it's over. I can't wait for you to see your new home. I know you'll be so happy there. But first, we have to take care of some business. Actually, that will work just fine for us all. I think we need to find a nice general store and pick out a few clothes. I don't think those coats you have will keep you very warm, and it looks like you could use some new shoes, gloves, and hats. It seems the orphanage committee discovered some hidden funds and has been kind enough to present us with enough money to see that you are equipped for the ride home. You'll need several things.

"Let's see, you must be Chloe, and the other girls are Eveline and Grace, right? You're Daniel and there's no doubt you two are Eli and Oliver, although, I'm not sure which is which."

The children stood quietly, seeming to be in complete awe.

"Franklin, if you'll be so kind as to help us into the carriage and find us a good store that carries merchandise at a decent price, then we'll be on our way. These children need proper clothing. Oh, forgive me," Letty said, turning toward the children, "are there any questions?"

"I don't understand this at all, if you live so far away, how did you know about us?" Chloe asked.

"I always wanted a large family and hoped for one," Letty said with a smile. "And hope is created by the good Lord. He hears our prayers and because of Him, hope often finds a way to grant your wishes and make your dreams come true. You must never give up. Hope is what keeps your dreams alive. I'll tell you all about it on the way home to our mountain."

Grace raised her hand shyly, though she still clung to Eveline.

"Child, you must learn to speak up," Letty said softly. "You needn't get permission to speak. That's a God given right. Just tell me. What would you like to know?"

Eveline stepped up and jutted out her little chin. "She wants to know what we're supposed to call you, ma'am?"

Letty smiled and glanced at Franklin. "That's a wonderful question, Grace. Thank you, Eveline, for helping her. Let me see. Now what should you call me? What would you like to call me? I have no preference. I'm open to suggestions?"

"We could call you Miss Wade like we called the ladies who worked at the orphanage," Chloe said, frowning.

"That sounds terribly formal," Letty replied. "Is that what you want to call me, Miss Wade?"

The six children thought for a minute and then shook their heads. Chloe spoke up, "If you adopted us then that make us sort of related now, right? I don't think Mama would be appropriate, though. Maybe we could, would you mind terribly if we called you *Aunt Letty*, or is that too much?"

Letty's face lit up and she nodded. "I like that. *Aunt Letty* sounds just fine. Aunt Letty it is. Now, I know there are lots of questions but I think they can wait until later when we can get comfortable and have a nice long talk. How about that shopping trip? Are you ready?"

The children grinned, nodded, and they were off.

~ * ~

Although Franklin admired and respected this hard-headed, determined, slightly crazy, mountain woman, he was relieved that those six children were not his. The

39

shopping trip proved to him that he was meant to either be childless, or that the woman he was about to marry would be in charge of their children, completely. He marveled at how efficient and in-charge Letty was. It took a good two hours to fit the children with shoes, coats, and find hats, gloves, and socks for each one. After paying for the clothes, Letty found she had enough money left to take them out for a good meal at a local café.

The children were excited beyond words. For one thing, they were hungry and for another, they had never eaten at a restaurant before. This was to be a great treat, even for Letty. She had, on occasion, eaten at the café in Kings Camp when the shopping had taken all day but it was rare.

~ * ~

After dropping Letty and the children off to eat, Franklin excused himself to prepare for the family gathering and the reading of the will. He told his driver to return to the restaurant, and when they had finished eating, deliver Letty and the children to the Browning residence and return to the office to pick up Franklin.

Back at the office, Franklin McDougan couldn't help but smile to himself as he placed the will, deeds, and a parcel into his satchel. During his career, Franklin executed hundreds of wills, drew up bequeaths to strange and unusual sources, but Patience's will had been a rare delight. She was a no-nonsense woman who knew her mind. She had provided her grandniece with a monthly sum that covered her expenses while she was there. All her debts had been paid before her death, and Franklin had received a handsome sum for his assistance. Only Franklin knew where Patience's money came from and she swore him to secrecy until the reading of the will.

~ * ~

Patience married the handsome young man, Henry, who stole her heart and set out to find riches lurking just over the next hill. He dreamed and searched, until his early death, for his pot of gold. Patience followed him to Seven Springs where, a few years later, he was shot by a disgruntled gambler. His belongings were returned to her and after the funeral she approached Franklin and showed him a paper she had found in her husband's traveling case.

The paper was a deed to a successfully active gold mine in California and that deed had made Patience a wealthy woman beyond her wildest dreams. The only downside was that her husband had never known what he had won or that he had been able to provide his dream for the woman he loved. She understood the mine was a legacy and was determined to see that it was only used for good. She swore Franklin to secrecy about the mine. No one was to know of her money or source of income until she was gone.

She bought a small cottage and lived there until her poor health forced her to move in with her grandniece. She sold the house and gave her niece, Chastity, a monthly allowance for her care.

~ * ~

A tap on the door brought Franklin back to the present. "Yes, who is it?" He called.

Joseph stuck his head through the doorway. "Just wondered, sir, if you wuz ready to leave?"

Franklin rose and chuckled. He was more than ready, he was looking forward to it.

~ * ~

Chastity and Cornelius ordered a grand buffet for the occasion. Cornelius's overdressed family filled the parlor and many of Chastity's cousins were there. The servants hovered around, anxious to satisfy their employers. Rumors started several weeks ago, when Chastity discovered that all Patience's bills were prepaid and her burial previously arranged and paid for. Whispered questions where she had gotten the money began to develop into rumors. Cornelius, a member of a prestigious men's club had also heard ru-

mors and talk of a gold mine deed passing hands had whet-
ted his appetite.

While waiting for the will to be read, he couldn't
help but greedily rub his hands together in anticipation of
the impending inheritance. "Darling," he whispered to
Chastity when she walked up beside him, "you've done a
magnificent job. The buffet looks mouthwatering and the
house is spotless."

Chastity beamed at her husband's compliment. "It
wasn't easy. The servants are absolutely helpless. I had to
direct every single task."

"Don't you worry your pretty little head, precious,"
he gushed. "After today, we'll hire the finest household
help money can buy. We'll be able to afford it once you receive your inheritance. After all we, er, *you* did for that
old mountain woman, you deserve every penny." Puffing
out his chest, Cornelius patted his wife's hand while his
guests milled around, looking properly mournful while filling their imported plates with food from the buffet.

The doorbell rang and Franklin arrived. After the
maid took his hat and coat, he approached Cornelius and
Chastity.

"Are you ready the read the will?" Cornelius asked
impatiently. "How long will this take? The old woman
didn't have any friends and we're her closest family. I
don't really see the need to drag this out too long."

Franklin clenched his fists and actually bit his tongue
to prevent the outburst that built within him. "This won't
take too long, Cornelius, I assure you.

"Chastity, do you have a place we can conduct our
business? It just has to be large enough for you, Cornelius,
Letty, and Dottie."

"What has Dottie got to do with this?" Cornelius
asked, his faced flushed with anger. "She's a simple-
minded servant."

"She was Miss Patience's personal maid and I'm sure
Patience left a little something to thank her for feeding,

bathing, and dressing her."

Cornelius made a guttural sound deep in his throat, frowned, and motioned to Franklin to follow Chastity who had headed across the hall to slide open a door. The room had been readied since the day Patience died and the chairs had been dusted that very morning just for the occasion.

"Has Miss Letty arrived?" Franklin asked, looking around the room.

"That woman showed up a short while ago with a half dozen, dirty, ragged, street urchins. They weren't dressed for the occasion and we felt she, and the children she had with her, would be more comfortable in a quiet place," Cornelius explained, sliding a glance at Chastity.

"I'm sure the children aren't trained in the art of proper behavior at delicate functions of this sort. Cornelius and I agreed they should remain in the kitchen," Chastity said.

"Wouldn't want the little tykes breaking our valuable, imported collectables, would we?" Cornelius added.

Franklin stiffened, narrowed his eyes at the couple, walked out the door and headed toward kitchen. He greeted the children warmly, offered Letty his arm, and escorted her into the library. His grin grew only larger when the servants ran to open the door for them.

~ * ~

After everyone was inside, Cornelius slid the two doors to the library shut and sat his chair behind Chastity, resting his hands on her shoulders. Cornelius was a local banker and acquired most of his money foreclosing on unfortunate men and women who had fallen on hard times. He obtained his position by succeeding his father who had taken over from his father. Cornelius had never broken a sweat in his life. He never even perspired unless he was about to close a big deal, or come into a large amount of money. Even then, it was not due to hard work, only greedy anticipation of becoming wealthier. Money was all he ever thought about and spent every minute figuring out how he could make more regardless of the consequences to his fellow man. Wealth was power and above all, Cornelius wanted power.

~ * ~

Once they were all settled, Franklin opened his case and took out his papers along with a package. He slowly spread the paper out, fanned out a few sheets, taking time to arrange them exactly to his liking. He also knew that prolonging the reading of the will, would be pure agony for Chastity and Cornelius. He opened the large packet and cleared his throat.

"Ladies and gentleman, this is the reading of the last will and testament of Patience Letitia Lawson, deceased. It may surprise you to learn that Mrs. Lawson was a very shrewd businesswoman and a very wealthy one. Her late husband left her a gold mine that is still producing high grade ore. She purchased hundreds of acres of mountain property in the area where she was born and raised, and provided her husband's family with enough money to live comfortably for the rest of their lives.

"I will not list all her generous gifts to hospitals, libraries, orphanages, or personal grants, but I will read the particular parts that concern her bequeaths to each of you."

Franklin adjusted his glasses and picked up the first paper. "To Chastity Browning, I leave the brooch her mother gave to me before she died and my thanks for allowing me to rent a room from her for which she was generously paid."

"That's all?" Chastity gasped and reached for Cornelius' hand for support.

He patted her absentmindedly. "Don't worry, dear, since I'm a businessman, I feel confident that she left the mine to me," he whispered, although Franklin heard him.

Franklin coughed slightly, smiled, and continued, "To Cornelius, I leave notice that I bought out his bank.

You foolishly sold shares to gullible, greedy friends, who didn't hesitate to sell you out for the all-mighty dollar. I paid off your house as well and gave your servants a handsome dismissal settlement since you can no longer afford to keep them on.

"Cornelius, you are a cruel and heartless man with no scruples or feelings. You have cheated, robbed, and stolen the very hope from the hearts of your fellow man in your gluttonous attempts to stuff you pockets with their money and property. You are a greedy and ruthless man and I hope you find a job with a kinder and more generous employer than you ever were. I'm sure that won't be hard."

Cornelius bellowed his rage and jumped to his feet, slinging his chair against the door. His face flushed a deep purple and his eyes bulged out. Sweat beaded on his upper lip and his entire body trembled with anger. "How dare that stupid old hillbilly," he screamed. "We took that witch in when she had no place to go, when she was old and sick and no one else would take care of her. I'll fight the will. I'll not stand for this. I want what's mine, that is, what's Chasity's." He yanked the doors open and stormed out, leaving Chasity to sit alone, stiff with indignation.

Franklin continued. "To Dorrie, my dear and sweet little helper, I leave five thousand dollars and my old cottage, which I bought for her. I know she has a sweetheart and perhaps now they can marry and have a family. I hope that this will give them a happy start for a new life."

Dorrie burst into tears, burying her face in her hands, repeating Patience's name over and over.

Franklin looked at Letty over the top of his glasses and watched her pat Dorrie's shoulder, and whisper comforting words in her ear, and then passed her a handkerchief.

"To Letty, my very best friend and devoted niece, who never failed to take me on a delightful journey each month. When I read her beautiful descriptions of the seasons, the land, and walked with her across the mountain through the pages of her letters, I was home. I mourned with her as each dear soul passed on to their just rewards and laughed at the antics of my friends. She helped keep this old mountain woman a young girl at heart. My family, friends, and devotion to my Maker are the most important things to me. To Letty, I leave my least important thing, but helpful nonetheless, the gold mine. Don't worry, dear Letty, the mine is being run by honest and capable men and Franklin sees to that. You needn't worry about the business end of the mine's operation, just enjoy the profits that will be deposited in your bank each month. I do ask you to do what you do best, give hope to those in despair, and think of me kindly in the coming years. We will meet again one day and I look forward to seeing you then."

Franklin removed his glasses, smiled, and looked up at the shocked face of Letty Wade. Her eyes were wide and disbelieving. Her mouth hung slack and she blinked wildly. She slowly raised her hand to her mouth and then her forehead.

"That, that can't be right, Mister McDougan," she gasped. "There must be some mistake. She can't have meant me. She just can't. Surely, she left it to someone else. Someone more deserving."

"No, Mrs. Wade, it's no mistake. Miss Patience and I talked for many, many long hours and discussed in length the details of her will. She generously paid Miss Chastity monthly fees for her room and board, and even gave her the profits from her house, which she bought back for Dorrie. She did not approve of Mister Browning's business dealing and was determined to stop him from ruining the lives of others.

"She left thousands of dollars to hospitals, libraries, and assorted other charitable organizations. She was very specific that you be the new owner of the mine. She did want me to advise you that no mine produces forever, therefore, you should be frugal and save a certain amount for the day when the mine gives out."

Chastity leaped shakily to her feet and snapped, "What kind of monthly profits will she be receiving? Those payments should be mine, after all, it was I who offered her my home, and it was I who saw to her day after day. She owes me, not her." She spat the words angrily and pointed her trembling finger at Letty. Tears made ugly trails down her heavily powdered face. Her fury was only equaled by her husband when he heard his legacy. She pushed herself from the chair, hands shaking, and stood behind the chair, gripping the back so hard her knuckles turned white.

Franklin smiled and looked at Letty. "Let me see," he murmured and shuffled through some papers. "I believe Miss Patience was receiving around five thousand dollars each month after all her bills were paid and assorted miscellaneous expenses were settled."

Letty moaned, her knees gave out, and Dorrie guided the chair under her. "F-f-ive th-th-... oh, my."

"That can't be," Chastity cried. "I just don't understand any of this. Why didn't she leave it to me?"

"Miss Patience said she only saw you once every three or four weeks and you acted like you hated being in the same room with her. She told me that Letty's letters were much more enjoyable than your visits, and longer, too."

"Oh," Chastity cried and buried her face in her hands, wailing. "It isn't fair," she sobbed. "It just isn't fair. I was her caregiver."

"Chastity, I'll be happy to share," Letty said softly. "You're absolutely right, it doesn't sound fair. I'll share the mine with you and Cornelius."

"I'm afraid not." Franklin shook his head. "The will states that neither Chastity nor her husband shall benefit from the money earned from the hard work of the men, not the ore from the mine, nor sweat of others. Sorry. By the way, she also left you the deed to all the mountain land

47

she bought. She felt you would keep the families safe."

"Out," Chastity screamed, stomping her foot, and wildly gesturing toward the door. "Get out of my house, now! You and those filthy urchins are not welcome. After all I did for that stupid old cow, for her to be so ungrateful. Cornelius was right. She was an old, old witch."

Letty rose and walked to the door unsteadily. Franklin glared at Chastity and swept his papers into his case.

"Miss Letty, if you'll gather the children, I'll meet you at the front door. We can stop by the bank and have your money transferred to the local bank near your home. You can draw out however much you need to buy extra supplies and prepare the children for the mountain.

"I have no idea what all you are going to need since children's needs are as foreign to me as raising chickens, and I have no idea how to raise chickens. I'll leave that sort of thing to you.

"I have a closed carriage and I'm going to have Joseph, my driver, take you and the children home. It's a mite cold to travel in an open wagon in this weather. You will be much more comfortable. I'll have another driver follow in your wagon. He can ride back with Joseph in the carriage. I'm sure Joseph will enjoy the company." He reached for her hand and saw she was gazing sadly at the floor.

"Letty, I must apologize for springing this on you without warning. I should have given you some idea of what you were in for, but Patience wanted it to be a surprise. "You must understand that this was her way of telling you how much she loved and trusted you. You have the children to think about now so try to pull yourself together."

She looked confused and still in a state of shock. She listened carefully to his instruction and when she started to protest, he shook his head, took her arm, and led her to the kitchen.

~ * ~

Her mind raced. She never dreamed of riches and certainly never prayed for them. She only asked the good Lord to keep her family and neighbors safe and healthy. She didn't know what to make of this blessing. She certainly would use it for the children, and see Patience's wishes carried out. She'd make sure each child received a good education and even attend the university if they wanted to, even the girls.

None of her neighbors would ever go hungry or be homeless and she would make sure that the people of the mountain were cared for. She smiled when she thought of the mountain. Now, she could start a school near her home for the children. Many of them never got an education due to the weather and the distance they had to travel to the schoolhouse in town. The time away from home traveling the long distance was something the families could not afford. The children were needed to help with the chores.

When she got her thoughts together and her emotions calmed, she would talk to Mr. McDougan about setting up a fund for the people on the mountain to utilize without it seeming like charity. They would never accept a hand out and she didn't blame them. She just wanted to share her good fortune with them and she was sure Franklin could help.

~ Three ~
Changes for Everyone

"Letty, you have money now. Enjoy a little treat now and then. Believe me, you can afford it. Your bank at home can advise you of how to open a savings account. I don't know the banker personally, but I'm sure he will try and talk you into all sorts of money making schemes. As your lawyer, if you want, I'll take care of that end of the business. After starting the savings account, you can keep a certain amount for daily expenses. Children don't come cheap, you know. This was all meant to happen, Letty. It was all meant to happen."

Letty walked into the kitchen and looked at the strained faces of the waiting children. They huddled together, although the kitchen was warm and cozy. Their eyes brightened at the sight of her and smiling, they jumped from their chairs.

"Children, let's go home," Letty said in a trembling voice. "The Lord has smiled upon us twice today, and it is a time to rejoice and what better place to do that but home on our beautiful mountain?"

Franklin drove them to the hotel where she quickly gathered her belongings. The children were still in a state of confusion and Letty wasn't sure how to explain what had just happened. She decided to wait they were on their way home.

The first stop was the bank, where with Franklin's help, she transferred a large sum of money to the Kings Camp Bank and withdrew five hundred dollars for expenses, at Franklin's suggestion. Letty had never seen five hundred dollars in her entire life and Franklin had to insist she take that amount. She would need it to clothe the children, buy supplies for the winter, and reminded that Christmas was not far off, she though what a lovely surprise she could give these children. A happy Christmas for the first time in years, or perhaps for the first time in their lives.

She signed a form allowing Franklin to pay taxes on the land, keep the accounts for her mine interests, plus invest the money that built up in the bank there. He was also to draw a monthly fee for his services.

The carriage arrived, the luggage stored, and Letty gave Franklin a warm hug before climbing inside for the long ride home. The attorney assured her that he would represent her interests and make sure her finances were taken care of. He had trusted her promise of sales from her jams and jellies, she now trusted him to manage her gift from Patience. She knew she made a dear friend in Franklin and it was nice to know he had been Patience's friend, too.

The carriage pulled away from the wooden sidewalk and they were on their way home to the mountains. Letty took her first deep breath since she had left the cabin. The past two days had exhausted her and she wanted nothing more than to see her cabin come into sight.

For the first ten minutes, the group traveled in complete silence. Everyone seemed uncomfortable and ill at ease. Letty thought hard as to what to say to relax and put them at ease.

"Daniel, have you always lived in Seven Springs?" Letty asked, trying to start conversation and ease the tension. I haven't been there, but once, several years ago when my aunt first moved there. I'm not very comfortable in town and especially cities, but I'm sure that some people like them very much and make themselves a very good home there.

"Uh, no, ma'am, we came from New York, where I was born. My Pa was uh, a carpenter and a friend of his was on his way to visit some relatives in Seven Springs. His friend was gonna look for a job that paid better than New York jobs, so Pa came down with his friend. Ma died and I went looking for Pa. He had written that he found a job in a coal mine, but when I got here, they told me he died in a cave-in. I tried to get back to New York but they were picking up kids that had no home, so I was put in the orphanage right after that."

"Eli, what about you and your brother?" she asked.

Eli glanced at Daniel. "We don't remember our parents. We lived with our aunt and uncle. They decided to go to California to look for gold. It was a long trip out there and, well, we were only two or three and they didn't want to take us. I remember hearing the lady say nobody would want twins." His chin trembled and he looked at Daniel. I just have to stay with my, my brother."

Letty clapped her hands together and stomped her feet.

"How lucky for me, I always wanted twins. I'm so glad you waited for me. Whatever would I do without you?" She chuckled and reached over and patted Oliver's knee.

Oliver smiled and nudged Eli. "We are lucky, too, aren't we, Eli?"

Eli ducked his head and grinned. "I guess so."

"Chloe, tell us about you girls," Letty said and untied her bonnet to pull it off.

"Our Mum died when Grace was born. Our Pa had left us long before that. I guess he went looking for work, too." She paused and looked toward Daniel who was staring out the window. "I tried to take care of us, but a neighbor turned us in to the police. They came one night and took us away." She cuddled the girls close to her and set her mouth in a determined line. "I promised them I would always look out for them and I will," she said softly and stuck out her chin defiantly.

"What fortunate little girls you are," Letty said to Grace and Eveline, "to have such a loving and devoted sister. I had two brothers, but they left home long ago. They, too, went off to find work. I'm not sure where they ended up. We got a couple of letters and then the letters stopped coming. I always hoped they'd come home one day. I guess I always will," she said softly.

"Aunt Letty?" Grace piped up, the first to call her by her new name. "Aunt Letty?" she repeated in a sing song voice.

It gave Letty a thrill to hear that sweet voice call her that. She looked at the tiny face, creased with a questioning look. "What, dear?" Letty asked.

"When you were in the bank, we were all talking about how strange you looked after going to that meeting with the big man and the fancy lady at the pretty house. Was it bad news? You looked so, so very surprised," she said shyly.

"Grace," Chloe said sharply. "You mustn't ask personal questions. I told you it was none of our business."

"Children, we mustn't have any secrets between us anymore. One person's problem will be a problem that will concern us all, and one person's joy will be a joy that we all will share. We'll share our business with the Lord and with each other. My business is your business, and whether you like it or not, your business is my business.

"That's what families are for and we are a family. It may take you a while to come to accept that, I understand, but it's a fact. We, now, are one family. For now and forever.

"I fully intended to tell you everything that happened in that meeting, as you call it. Actually, it was the reading of a will. A will is a piece of paper that someone writes before they die to make sure that the things they own will be given to the people that they want to have them.

"I came here to attend the funeral of my Aunt Patience. I loved her very much. She was my mother's sister, the last family member I had, but now I have you. The man that helped us and read Aunt Patience's will is Mister Franklin McDougan. He was her lawyer and now he is ours and he is also is our friend. The reason I looked so strange is I found out that Aunt Patience left me, or rather, *us* a gold mine. I was just flabbergasted when I found out.

That's why I must have looked so, what did you say, Grace, surprise? Yes, indeed, that's what I was all right, surprised."

"A gold mine?" Daniel yelped. "A gold mine?" Then, suddenly his face fell. "It's probably a dud. Pa used to say that most good things are duds."

"What's a dud?" Eli asked, frowning.

"That means the mine is a hole in the ground with nothing in it. Lots of people dig for gold. Lots of people have mines. That doesn't mean there's any gold," Daniel said dejectedly. "I wouldn't count on it having any gold left. They probably got all the gold out and then sold it."

Letty listened quietly until he finished. When they were quiet, she smiled. "Ours isn't a dud, Daniel. Ours is an honest to goodness, real life, gold-producing mine. We will have money in the bank from that mine every month for a while. Now, it may be a dud someday, but for right now, it's got gold. If we're careful, we'll have all the money we need when it finally does play out."

The children thought about what she said and one by one began to smile, and their eyes lit up.

"Wow," Oliver said, "a gold mine, a real gold mine. Is it around here, Aunt Letty? Can we see it, can we, please?"

"No, Oliver, it's in California. My Aunt Patience has reliable men running it. Mister McDougan is going to take care of it for us. He's a good man, Mister McDougan is, and I want you all to remember that. He was the man who helped me get all of you. If it hadn't been for him getting all the paperwork, locating all the right people, and getting their signatures, we wouldn't be together right now. We owe him more than we can ever pay. He's a good friend to me, and to you. We must remember to include him in our prayers at night," Letty said with a smile.

"Will you teach us?" Eveline asked, looking up through long, dark lashes at Letty.

"Teach you what, dear?" Letty asked gently.

"Will you teach us how to do prayers?" She blushed and dropped her head. "I kinda 'member Mama saying prayers when I was a little girl but I forget what you're supposed to do or say."

Tears filled Letty's eyes. She reached over and took Eveline's hand. "Oh, yes, I'll be happy to teach you to say prayers. It's really very easy, you know. You just have to talk to God. Tell Him your problems and tell Him your joys. He wants to hear from you, from all of you. He's your heavenly Father and you talk to Him just like you to talk to me. I'll show you."

~ * ~

Just before dark, the horses slowed and the carriage stopped in a small town for the night. The driver pulled up to the blacksmith shop and made arrangements to board the horses. The weather again, looked stormy.

Letty told the drivers to feed and water the horses and meet them later at the hotel restaurant for supper. She took the children to the hotel, found rooms for the two drivers, herself, and the children before going to the dining room to order them something to eat. The children walked in quietly, and nervously looked around at the other customers.

The drivers joined them. One introduced himself as Joseph Clark, and in turn, introduced Stan Oakley, thanking Letty for the invitation.

"Aunt Letty, what are we supposed to do now?" Daniel asked, looking at the menu.

"Would you all like me to order for you?" Letty asked, glancing at the children. When they all nodded, she studied the menu and when the waiter returned, she waited until after the drivers ordered.

"I would like to have seven plates of the fried chicken, buttered potatoes, green beans and gravy. Please bring six glasses of milk and I'd like a cup of coffee."

The waiter scribbled down the order, nodding while he wrote. "Will there be anything else? We have a lovely dessert cart you can choose from."

"Let's get supper eaten first, young man," Letty replied.

"Yes, ma'am." The waiter gave a nod and hurried to fill the order.

Joseph and Letty chatted about the weather, Seven Springs, and Franklin McDougan, whom Joseph had worked for for ten years. Letty asked Stan about his family and told him how much she appreciated his help. Occasionally, they asked the children questions just to include them in the conversation, but the children were shy and didn't have much to say.

The waiter arrived with the food and when it was all placed in front of the group, Letty bowed her head. Everyone followed her example and Letty said grace. "Lord, we thank you for all your blessings and for bringing us together. Thank you for the food you have provided, and watch over us and guide us in our daily lives. Amen."

The drivers mumbled "Amen," and the children echoed them. Letty looked up and saw the children eyeing the plates before them,

"All right, children, eat up and let's remember our manners." Letty smiled when each child shyly reached for a fork and took their first bite.

The look of delight on their faces brought tears to Letty's eyes and made her wonder when they had last eaten a good meal. Letty nibbled her food while watching her new family eat, smile, and eat again. She felt so blessed. After the children had finished, they laughingly moaned with overstuffed stomachs. Letty paid for the meal, collected the keys, and gave Joseph the key for him and the wagon driver. She settled the boys in one room, the girls in another, and finally closed the door to her room, collapsing on the bed. She couldn't remember being so tired, even after a long day of hoeing and weeding at home.

Finally, she stood and struggled out of her dress and

shoes, and slipped her gown on over her head. The children had to sleep in their underwear, but didn't seem to mind. She guessed they were used to it. But tonight, they would not be sleeping in the cold. Tonight, they had blankets and heat. Things would change for these precious charges. Yes, things would change soon. As exhaustion overtook her, she climbed into bed and closed her eyes, and took a deep breath. The very last thing she remember- ed was mumbling a quick prayer and sliding her feet under the covers.

"Aunt Letty, Aunt Letty!"

Letty was jerked back to reality the next morning by a loud voice, a frantic rap on her door, and the rattling of the doorknob.

"Aunt Letty. Aunt Letty, come quick, Daniel is under the bed and won't come out. Eli and Oliver don't know what to do. Aunt Letty?" Chloe stood shivering in her underclothes.

Letty struggled out from under the covers and pulled on her robe. She ran to the door, twisted the key, and raced down the hall to the open door where Eli and Oliver stood wide-eyed and frightened.

"In there," Eli pointed. "Under the bed. I don't know what's wrong. He won't answer or come out. He might be dead. Do you think he's dead?" Eli pointed to the bed where the covers had been pulled off and were sticking out from under the bed.

Letty approached slowly and carefully got on her hands and knees. Her joints pained acutely, she grimaced and peered under the foot of the bed. "Daniel, dear, do you need any help? Is there anything I can do? Have you lost something? Daniel, we're all here. Do you need anything?"

There was no answer.

Letty spoke louder. "Daniel, talk to me, dear. Can you hear me? Is there anything I can do?"

Silence.

Letty struggled upright and walked back to the door.

She shooed everyone out, told the girls to take the boys to their room and wait. "Chloe, dear, you all get dressed and close the door. The boys can dress in just a moment."

Returning to the bed, she leaned over and called again. "Daniel? Daniel, its Aunt Letty. It's time to get up, get dressed, and go home."

"Who's there?" a muffled, sleepy voice answered.

"Daniel, honey, it's Aunt Letty. It's time to go home. You must come out from under there. Do you need any help?"

"Aunt Letty?" There was a loud thump and the bed shook.

"Ouch. Where am I? What am I doing down here? Ouch," he exclaimed, bumping his head again.

Once again, Letty lowered herself painfully to the floor. She thought carefully before answering. "I think you must have dropped something on the floor and fell asleep when you went to look for it"

Daniel's head appeared from under the edge of the bed and wormed his way through the covers and stiffly got to his feet. He reached for Letty's arm and helped her up. Daniel rubbed his face roughly and ran his fingers through his hair. He looked around wildly.

"Where are the twins? What happened to Eli and Oliver? Aunt Letty, they're not here."

"They're fine," she assured him. "They're in the room with the girls. "They were frightened when they found you under the bed. They really need to come in and get dressed. Are you okay?"

Daniel grinned awkwardly. "Sure, but first, I might as well tell you. I didn't fall asleep looking for something. I've done this before. I don't know why, Aunt Letty, but I, I walk around sometimes in my sleep. Not often, mind you, but I have woken up in strange places. I'm sorry if I frightened anyone. If it's gonna be a problem then—"

"Problem? Nonsense. It just shows that you have a great imagination for adventure. Maybe when you get a

58

chance to have real honest-to-goodness adventures, you won't have to do them in your sleep.

Now, help the boys get dressed and we'll have some breakfast. We need to get home. I think home is the answer to everything." She pulled him to her, hugged him tight, and hurried out before she embarrassed him further.

After a filling breakfast of sugary porridge with rich cream, toast, jam, and hot tea, the group started off on the last leg of the trip home. Snow fell lightly but the wind had calmed.

Letty entertained the children with stories of the cabin and the mountains. She told them of the owl in the barn and the red-tailed hawk living in the attic. She described the deer in the meadows, the elk on the hillside, and the squirrels in the forest, but decided she'd wait until later to tell them about the wild boars, coyotes, bobcats and black bears. Soon, she would give them the rules for exploring the area safely. The children needed to know the beauty and delight of the mountain now, not frighten them to death with tales of vicious creatures.

Joseph pulled the carriage to a halt, opened the roof door and called down, "Mrs. Wade, we're coming into Kings Camp, did you want to stop anywhere before I take you home?"

"Oh, yes, thank you, Joseph. We need to get the children some clothes. There's a general store in the middle of town. Do you mind if we stop there?" she asked.

Joseph grinned and shook his head. "Ma'am, my time is your time. I will stop anywhere you need to. Mister McDougan has already generously paid me to see to your every need until I deposit you at your front door."

"Now, don't that just beat all? Thank you, Joseph, let's get to the store. We've got clothes to buy."

Floyd Cramer, owner of Cramer's Mercantile, rushed to wait on Letty. He smiled from ear to ear but the smile froze when he saw six raggedy children standing behind her looking around the store. Grace reached toward the table causing Floyd's demeanor to change. He stiffened and shook his finger at the child.

"Here now," he bellowed. "What are you all doing there? Git. Don't you young'uns touch anything. Where did you come from? Excuse me a moment, Miss Letty. Who do you belong to? Where's your ma or pa?" His face twisted in anger and he snarled, grabbing Eli's sleeve.

Letty reached out and snatched Floyd by the collar in mid-stride, causing him to gag at the sudden stop.

"They belong to me, Floyd Cramer, and I'd hate to take my business all the way to Beaver Cap because of the rude, disrespectful way you treat my children," she snapped.

"Y-y-your children?" Floyd stammered, his mouth gasping like a fresh hooked fish. "Miss Letty, when did you, uh, I didn't know you had children."

"I guess you don't know everything then, do you? You're the second person I've met lately that has that problem. I know you wouldn't want your children treated the way you just treated mine now, would you?" she said sharply.

Floyd shook his head. Other customers gathered around and listened intently.

Letty walked over to the children, who had backed up against the wall. "This is Chloe, Eveline, and the little one is Grace. The boys are Daniel, and the twins are Eli and Oliver. Later in the spring, they will, from time to time, come in here to pick up various items for me and I expect you to treat them with the utmost courtesy. Otherwise, old friend, I will take my business elsewhere. Do I make myself clear?"

Floyd swallowed hard and nodded nervously.

"Good. Chloe, pick out three dresses each for the girls and yourself and you'll need three pairs of boy's pants, heavy shirts, underwear, along with a couple of gowns. Daniel, you and the boys select one pair of dress pants and a good shirt, and four pair of work pants, heavy-duty shirts, underwear, and night shirts. All of you pick out six pairs of socks and make sure they're nice and warm. We'll get cooler wear for the summer next spring. It's hard washing in freezing weather and I don't want you wearing dirty clothes all winter. I'll check over what you pick out. Hurry now, Joseph's waiting."

"Just how do you intend to pay for this, Miss Letty?" Floyd asked nervously. "I still have some of your jellies and jams from the last time you were in. Do you have something different to trade for what you need?" He looked anxiously at the growing pile of clothes.

Letty Wade had been a customer when he was a young man and although he didn't want to insult her, he couldn't imagine how this poor woman expected to be allowed to charge this large amount. It would take forever for her to pay off this charge. He didn't want to be rude, but business was business.

"No, Floyd, I don't have anything to trade today, but don't you worry. We'll be paying cash today. I also want to settle up my account, if I still have anything outstanding on your books." Letty calmly reached into her bag for her change purse. She had cleverly separated her money into several small amounts and placed them in different areas. Some were hidden on her person, some in her shoe, and some, she left in her purse. Letty was a mountain woman, but she was far from stupid.

"Miss Letty, I'm not sure you realize how much all this totals up to. If you eliminate many of the items on the list and limit the children to one set of clothes, I will be happy to put them on a charge for you." Floyd noted for the first time, the crowd of eavesdropping customers gathering with interest.

"Thank you, Floyd. I appreciate your giving me credit in the past, but I'll be paying in cash today."

Floyd's jaw dropped and the people standing around

began to whisper to one another. The whispering spread throughout the store, sounding like a swarm of buzzing bees.

"I sold some jam and jelly in the city, Floyd," she fibbed. "Could you add up what we've bought and just fill this list I have? We'll be taking the clothes with us and you can put the other supplies in the wagon when it arrives.

"Aren't you in your wagon, Miss Letty?" Floyd strained to look out the front window.

"We're in a big carriage parked down the street," Eveline piped up. "Our wagon will be here later."

"Children, please concentrate on choosing your clothing and finish shopping," Letty said.

"It was too cold for the children to travel in the wagon," she explained to Floyd. "A friend loaned us his carriage and another drove our wagon."

When Grace opened her mouth, Chloe covered it with her hand. "Shh. Aunt Letty knows what she's doing. Everybody hush and take your clothes to the counter."

Silently, they filed to the register and stood politely quiet and reserved wile Letty approved their selections. Floyd added everything up, Letty paid for the clothes, the things she had charged earlier, and the supplies she had just bought. One of the clerks gathered up her purchases and headed outside to load them in her carriage and Letty handed each of the children a coin.

"I'll bet if you look really hard, you can find something that you would like to buy. Take your time, we've got a little while to get home before dark. Enjoy yourselves, children, spend wisely, and join me at the door when you've paid for your purchases."

The children looked in amazement at the coins she had just handed them. They had never been given money to spend on just themselves, to buy anything they wanted, whether it was good for them or not. At first, they just stood there until Eli gave a whoop and headed for the candy counter with Oliver at his heels. Chloe walked to a nearby table and picked up a pad of paper and a stick of charcoal, while Grace and Eveline looked through a stack of books on a counter. Daniel thought for a moment longer and walked quietly to the counter and asked Floyd's wife something secretively. She nodded, smiled, and disappeared around the counter toward the corner.

Soon, all the children were standing beside Letty at the door and Joseph opened the carriage when he saw them exit. He helped them all in, climbed onto the driver's seat, flicked the reins, and urged the team down the road.

Inside the coach, Eli and Oliver held their brown paper bags out to everyone. "Help yourself," Eli said proudly. "I've got lemon drops and Ollie's got peanut brittle."

"Look at our picture books." Grace eagerly held up her book, and Eveline joined her. "The man said they were second-hand but they're new to me. Books are new to anyone who hasn't read them. You can look at them anytime."

"I bought some paper and charcoal," Chloe said shyly. "Any of you can use it to draw a picture."

"Daniel, what did you get?" Oliver asked.

Daniel grinned uncomfortably and opened his bag. "I got some ribbons for the girls, two whistles for the twins, and I got a comb for, um, for Aunt Letty," he murmured.

"What did you get for yourself?" Chloe asked.

"I thought about it and I couldn't think of a thing I wanted except to buy you all something. I remember Ma saying that it was better to give than to receive, and that giving was a blessing. I feel we are all so blessed today. Thank you, Aunt Letty, for letting us all stay together. I was worried that, that..." Tears welled up in his eyes and the other children looked like they were about to join in.

Letty jumped in. "I think you all made excellent choices in your spending. I'm so proud of you children, I don't know what to say. We are indeed blessed, every one of us, and this is just the beginning of a wonderful life on the mountain. All of us together for always." When she felt tears burning her eyes, she quickly turned away and grabbed Grace's book.

"Let's see your book, Grace. You are absolutely right, second-hand books have new stories if you haven't read them. Maybe I'll read a few pages while we travel. That will help pass the time away." Letty read while the children listened and looked out the window at the hills, forests, and meadows drifting past.

~ * ~

Daniel stopped his tears and relaxed while he watched his brothers munch their candy and his sisters admire their ribbons. The worries that kept him awake so many nights in the past, the cold beds, and the thin appearance of his little family, now seemed a lifetime away.

His mother would be so proud they had all been able to stay together, and his Pa, who died trying to make a living, drifted through his thoughts. Life had been hard on them and hopefully, those days were over. For the first time in years, Daniel had hope, and he remembered what Aunt Letty said the first time he had met her.

"Hope is what keeps dreams alive."

How right she had been. He had new hope, and now he was beginning to develop dreams. Dreams of seeing the girls grow up beautiful, healthy, happy, and someday marry and raise children. Dreams of seeing the twins go off and become successful businessmen. No longer did he feel those dreams were foolish but now, they were possible. He took a deep breath and smiled at Chloe, who was looking at him and probably thinking the same thing he was. They always had been uncannily alike in their thoughts.

~Four~
Secrets Revealed

*A*fter she read awhile, Letty put the book down and looked at her little charges. They were so young, so inno-cent, and already she loved them so much. However, it was never too early to begin a learning process.

"I need to tell you all a few things, children. One thing is, you are never, never to tell people about the gold mine. There are several reasons. First, pride is a sin. Sec-ond, there are people out there who wouldn't hesitate for a second to rob or cheat you out of your money. Hopefully, no one will ever know about the mine. Aunt Patience never told anyone about it except Franklin, and that was a very good thing. People treat you differently when they think you have money. They never reveal their true selves. They may pretend to be your friend when they're really not. Aunt Patience trusted us with the responsibility of the mine and now that must be our secret. Do you understand?"

The children listened solemnly, nodding vigorously when she was finished.

~ * ~

Joseph drove out of town and took the side road Let-ty had instructed him. The road began to gently rise and soon they were headed toward the cabin. Joseph promised to tap on the roof if he saw anything he thought might in-terest the children. He let the horses follow the road and looked intently at the beautiful scenery around him. There was no doubt in his mind why Mrs. Letty Wade loved her home so deeply. He smiled at the thought of waking up every morning and looking out over the mountains each day.

~ * ~

A sudden tap on the roof sent the children lunging for the windows. Daniel stuck out his head and looked up toward Joseph, who pointed to the left. When he turned to

65

the left, he froze. In a meadow, seven or eight deer pawed at the snow covered clumps of grass while a large antlered buck stood guard. His head held high, and although he spotted the carriage, he detected no threat and did not warn the others to flee.

"Look, children, look." Letty pointed out the window and saw a second small family of deer grazing in the meadow by the road. The sheer amazement on the children's faces told Letty that the mountain held untold treasures waiting to be discovered.

"How much farther?" Eli asked, fidgeting around.

"Not long, dear," Letty said with a smile. "Are you in a hurry or can you wait about half an hour?"

"I'll try to wait." He ducked his head self-consciously, blushing when Daniel grinned at him and ruffled his hair

"Oh, Aunt Letty, look," Chloe cried.

When they made a sharp turn, the landscape became a pure white scene. Snow fell heavier now and icicles draped each limb and leaf, making everything look like a fantasy picture in crystal. A brook running along the road had frozen over and the water beneath shimmered and sparkled like mirrors in the sun. The day faded quickly and the world around them seemed to be hidden in fluffy clouds with diamonds and crystals leading them home. It felt like the mountain welcomed them home by presenting them with a special attraction.

"It's so beautiful," Eveline sighed. "I didn't realize that the world could be so pretty."

The road narrowed and the meadow seemed to be swallowed up by thick woods on each side. The carriage seemed enveloped in darkness for a few minutes before the trees thinned out and Joseph tapped again. Before they could look, the carriage made a swing around and stopped.

"Children, we're home," Letty whispered.

Immediately, both doors swung open and the children scrambled from the carriage and stared around the clearing and at the cabin.

"It's so big, Aunt Letty. When you said a cabin, I thought of a little log house. It's so big," Chloe repeated.

"Yes, it's a fairly good size. When I was a young woman, I lived here with my husband, my ma and pa, my grandparents too, and we had plenty of room. When it was just me here, I think the house grew lonely for company. It wasn't used to having just one silly old woman to keep warm and dry. It always needed more people. I think it needed children." She chuckled and pushed them toward the door.

"Joseph, won't you and Stan come in and have a cup of coffee? I know you must be cold," Letty said.

"I'll help you get your things in and start a good fire up and maybe I *will* have a cup. Stan should be here soon with the wagon and supplies. After we unload, we'll put your wagon up, water and feed all your animals, have that coffee, and drive on back into town for the night."

Within the hour, Eli had used the outhouse and was more comfortable, the fireplace burned brightly, the wood stove radiated heat, and coffee perked.

Joseph brought in the luggage and packages, and assisted Stan in unloading the supplies Letty ordered from the store. They backed the wagon into the shed, unhitched the horses, fed them, and were soon ready for a hot cup of coffee.

"Ma'am, this is one fine house you have here," Stan said admiringly.

"Thank you, Mister Oakley. My late husband added several rooms, and the second floor, the first year we were married. I lived here with him, my parents and their parents. This house was his pride and joy. He made sure there wasn't any space for the winter wind to come through and even built a fireplace upstairs. I was very proud of him, and proud of this house. I think he did a wonderful job."

"Indeed he did, ma'am. I've never seen finer carpenter, or joiner, work in all my days. He was a fine craftsman, ma'am, a fine craftsman. This house is excel-

67

lent."

Letty smiled at the compliments. She knew Frank would be so pleased that his work impressed people. He worked so hard on the house so it would be Letty's dream home.

The drivers declined Letty's offer of supper and after they drank several cups of coffee, Joseph and Norton told the family goodbye and accepted everyone's thanks. The night was quiet and still. The snow had stopped and the moon worked hard to peep through clouds and shed some light.

~ * ~

Letty sliced some bread and placed the slices over a grill in the fireplace. She scrambled a dozen eggs and placed jams and jellies on the table. She looked at the jars of preserves and thought that the last time she had used them was when she left for the funeral. Little did she know then that the next time those jams would be used, there would be six pairs of little hands grabbing for them.

After supper, Letty went upstairs to help the children get settled. Letty had been using the downstairs bedroom and all the furniture in the upstairs rooms were draped in dust covers. In a short while they had all been removed, the tables dusted, the floor swept, and the lamps brightly lit.

The girls asked if they could share a room, and Eli and Oliver wanted Daniel to stay in their room, at least for a while, they said. He was happy to comply.

Chloe picked out a large front bedroom for her and the girls, while the boys wanted one in the back so they could look out at the trees. Once the dust covers were removed and the beds had fresh linens on them, the children unwrapped the packages containing their new clothes and put them in their chest of drawers and hung their dresses on hooks, while placing shirts and pants on the shelves of their closets. The lamps were turned down, and Letty showed them how to kneel by their beds, place their hands

68

together, and taught them their first prayer.

In each room she had them repeat after her. "Lord, we thank you for this day and all our blessings. Watch over us and Mister McDougan, and lead Mister Joseph and Mister Oakley safely home. Be with us while we dream and guide us when we wake. Amen."

When they were all in bed, she tucked each one in and kissed them on the forehead. She blew out their lamps and left each of the doors open a just crack.

At the boys' door, she joked, "Wait and have your adventure in the morning, Daniel. I'm really tired tonight."

"Yes, ma'am," he said and grinned. "I'll try. I'm pretty tired, too and right now I don't feel like sleepwalking."

"I'll need help at breakfast girls, I'm sure I can count on you to hurry down and help me."

"Yes, ma'am, Aunt Letty," they chorused.

Downstairs, she cleaned the plates and set out scraps by the fence. She washed up the dishes, banked the fire, and took the lamp into her room. On her dresser, near the picture of Patience, sat a framed photograph of Frank a traveling photographer had taken shortly after they were married. In the picture he was smiling. But, as she thought back, Frank always smiled.

She washed up, changed into her gown, said her prayers, kissed Frank's picture, and stiffly climbed up onto the tall bed, sinking deep in the down-filled mattress.

"Oh, Lord," she whispered. "What have I done to myself and this mountain? There will be changes that I'm not sure we are prepared for. Except for a baby or two, now and then, this old mountain hasn't seen much change. Are we strong enough to handle it? I need to do this right. I need to say all the right things, listen when I should, and be able to discipline properly.

"I have given myself a very great responsibility for an old woman my age without considering the fact that I've no experience in what I'm about to undertake. I've pushed myself the past few days, I know, but I need You to give me the strength to raise these children, guide them to do Thy will, show them how to build a good life, and most of all, teach them to trust and love once more. Thank you, Lord. Amen."

Letty took a deep breath and when she closed her eyes, she felt a slight tingle start at her head and travel down her body to her toes. It felt good. It made her feel happy. Thinking it was just a winter chill, she turned over, smiled, cuddled down, and was soon fast asleep.

~ * ~

During the next few days, the children learned all about chores and the everyday routine of living on the mountain. Letty showed them the smokehouse, describing all the hanging meat, and what piece was used for what. She showed them the wood pile and told them how important it was to keep it cut and stacked to use. Most of it was stored behind the chicken house and all they needed to do was transfer it to the wood box built into the kitchen wall.

She assigned the chickens to Eveline and Grace. Grace fed the chickens and Eveline gathered the eggs. They were also to check and make sure the fencing was secure so the chickens would be safe from coyotes, bobcats, and foxes. Daniel and the twins were in charge of the barn animals. Daniel would make sure the horses had grain and the cow was fed and the stalls were kept clean and, she added, the twins were to help him do all that. Chloe's chores were gathering vegetables from the fruit cellar and setting out the after-meal scraps for the hungry forest critters. Letty told them that raccoons and possums waited anxiously each night regularly for their supper and if ignored, would try to get inside. She explained what a mess they could make in the house and nobody wanted that.

On clear days, Letty took them for long walks to the meadow, through the woods, and along the streams down to the small lake. She taught them to identify tracks, dens, and warned them against trying to make friends with animals. She explained as carefully as she knew how that most animals didn't mind interacting with humans on a small level, but they needed their freedom and their own space. She warned them not to pick up baby animals for their mothers were probably not far off and became enraged whenever they thought their offspring was in danger and to many wild creatures, humans meant danger. The children nodded and agreed to heed her warnings. She went on to inform them that if they ever found an animal hurt or injured in any way, they were not to touch it, but to come and get her immediately and she would take care of it.

No child was to go out alone. Each had to take a buddy with them. If they went into the woods they were to tie rags along the path to guide them back and if they went up the mountain, they were to stay on the trail and not wander off and get lost. It was a beautiful world to explore, but could be dangerous if they were careless.

Within a month, it was as if they had always been together. Daniel had a couple of sleepwalking episodes the first week, but they stopped when his full days gave him deep, restful sleep. The twins were full of boundless energy and Letty sometimes wished she had the power to slow them down just a bit. Chloe was a born homemaker. She lived for Letty's cooking lessons, while Eveline and Grace enjoyed sewing and playing with the chickens. They spent an hour feeding them and gathering eggs. They already named each hen, but called the rooster *Hateful*, since he objected to their intrusion and did his best to drive them out of the chicken pen every chance he got. He wasn't used to competition and was as mean as bear with a thorn in his paw.

One day when Letty was taking inventory of the supplies, she realized it was the first week of December and Christmas wasn't far off. She hadn't had a Christmas tree since her parents passed away, nor had she celebrated the holiday except in her prayers on Christmas morning with a Bible reading. The children hadn't mentioned it and she wondered if they had even been allowed to celebrate when they were in the orphanage. Surely, some group or other had taken gifts to the children there. Even in Kings Camp, no family in need was overlooked. She wasn't sure how to bring the subject up so they wouldn't be uncomfortable. This is something she would have to think about.

Letty didn't have to think very long. Mid-morning the very next day, while making a list of the jars of fruit, jams, and jellies in the pantry, the door burst open. Eli stood panting in the doorway, his eyes bulging, his mouth hanging open, and tears gathered in his eyes. His mouth opened and closed several times. "S-s-someone's c-c-coming," he gasped.

"Calm down, Eli, speak slowly," Letty coaxed him.

Eli took a deep breath and started again. "Some-one's coming up the road, Aunt Letty. Do you think they're coming to take us away? Don't let them take us, Aunt Let-ty, please, don't let them. We're happy here."

Grace and Eveline came into the room and Grace began to cry when she saw Eli's distress. "What's wrong?" she cried. "Are they taking us away?"

"Whoa. Everybody calm down. Eli, Grace, nobody's going to take anybody away. What makes you think that?" She gathered him to her and rocked him to and fro as Chloe held Grace. Her heart broke at the fear they lived in and must have lived in for several years.

"B-b-because they always do," he sobbed.

"Not this time, little one, not this time, and not ever again," she added. "Aunt Letty won't ever let that happen. Don't you know that? That's why I came and got you, so I can watch over and keep people from just taking you off. You must believe me, little one, you're here to stay."

She took Eli by the shoulders and led him over to Chloe who put an arm around him. She felt his pain and his fear. Unconvinced, Eli hid his face on Chloe's shoulder.

Letty grabbed her heavy shawl, threw it over her shoulders, and walked onto the porch to greet their visitor and see just what was going on. At first, she couldn't believe her eyes, and then she realized Eli's concern. It was Joseph, driving the same carriage that brought them to the cabin. Eli was afraid it was here to carry them away. She had to admit, the sight of that carriage made her stomach quiver just a bit.

Joseph waved as soon as he saw her and a grin broke out across his face. "Merry Christmas, Miss Letty," he shouted.

She nodded, still confused as to why Joseph should be here. Her confusion increased when she saw Franklin McDougan leaning out the window smiling and waving gaily to Daniel, Oliver and herself. "Merry Christmas, children."

Daniel and Oliver stood frozen by the barn. They, too, were fearful of this visitor, even if Aunt Letty said he was a good man. They hadn't yet learned to trust people just because they were told someone was a good man.

Franklin leaped out of the coach and grabbed Letty's hand before she could speak. He kissed both cheeks and guided her back into the house by her arm.

"Chloe, please ask Joseph to join us in the house after he has settled the horses, will you, please?" Franklin asked. "Letty, have you got some of that strong mountain brewed coffee on the stove? I would love a cup to warm me up."

Letty shook her head. "No, but let me put on a fresh pot. I could use a cup, too. I hope there's no trouble. What brings you so far from Seven Springs, Mister McDougan?"

"As your attorney, I feel I should keep you regularly informed of your financial status and when I run across valuable information concerning you and your lovely family, it's my duty to tell you and this needed to be said face-to-face."

"That's very kind of you, Mis—"

"Please, call me Franklin, Miss Letty, your aunt did. I

73

feel we are slightly related through Patience."

"Thank you, er, Franklin, but you could have sent a letter. If I receive any mail marked urgent, they usually send somebody to bring it to me."

"Not this. Please, let's wait until the coffee's ready, besides, Joseph was instrumental in obtaining this bit of news," he said slyly.

A rap on the door and Joseph entered with Daniel and Oliver by his side. "I think that he should be the one to inform you of this interesting development," Franklin said.

"I 'preciate the invite," Joseph murmured.

"Please have a seat at the table, Joseph. The coffee will be ready in a minute or two." Letty got down her company cups. Over the years, an assortment of dishware had been collected by three generations of Letty's family. There were the everyday dishes, those were used for ordinary meals, and then there was a sixteen place setting of matched dishes that Letty's grandmother had brought when she married. They were only used for special days, holidays, or when they had visitors. Today was for visitors. She had a feeling it was going to end up being a special day.

Chloe placed the sugar bowl and a small pitcher of cream on the table and Eveline put out a plate of cookies. The children rushed about trying to please, and yet, go unnoticed. When the table was prepared, they backed up against the wall and stared at Joseph and Franklin, fear still shadowed their eyes.

Letty poured the coffee and sat down at the end of the table. She glanced over at the children and seeing how uneasy they were, she thought perhaps if she could get them busy.

"Children, why don't you go read a bit, while Mister McDougan and I talk?" Letty said gently.

"Miss Letty, I think they should stay. What we've got to say concerns you all," Franklin said softly.

"We're not going back, we won't!" Eli hid behind Daniel.

"No!" Grace hid her face and sobbed. "Aunt Letty, don't let them take us."

"No, no," Franklin assured them. "That will never happen. I have good news, do you hear me? *Good news*. Oh, my goodness. I haven't done this very well. I certainly hope I learn in time to handle young ones a bit better than I do now. Please sit down here with us. I have some questions to ask you and then I'll tell you everything, I promise."

Eli still stuck tight to Daniel, Grace had stopped sobbing, but was still sniffling loudly. They all sat down close to Letty, crowding around her like frightened chicks around a mother hen. She tried to reach out and touch each one to reassure them of what Franklin and she had told them. They were safe there with her on the mountain.

"Daniel, how old are you?" Franklin asked gently.

"I'm eight, the same as Chloe," he stated firmly.

"No, you're not. You're eleven and Chloe is twelve," Franklin corrected.

"No, I—"

"Daniel, I know everything," Franklin said and reached over and patted his hand. "And don't you worry, it's all right."

"Letty, do you recognize this?" Franklin held out a small polished clay disc with a rawhide cord running through a small hole.

With trembling hands, Letty reached out and took the disc. "Where? Uh, where did you get this? It's a hawk amulet and it belonged to my one of my brothers. Both had one just like it. Pa gave it to them before they left. See." She shakily pointed to the carved feature. "See the hawk in the middle? My brothers loved hawks. Where on this sweet earth did you get this, Franklin?"

"Let me turn the talking over to Joseph. This is where he comes in. He's the man with the firsthand information. Tell them what all you found, Joseph."

"Miss Letty," Joseph's face beamed, "when I got back to Seven Springs, I put the carriage up, and went by the orphanage to see if Daisy, that is, Miss Epperson, need-ed any help moving. When I got there, she was gone but a couple of workers were there and they had two boxes of stuff they'd found layin' around in the office area when they went through the building. I took it straight away to Daisy, er, Miss Epperson's. I thought they might be im-portant. She went through them and put several things in a pile and said they belong to the Walker children.

"At first, I didn't know who she was talking about, but she said, "It belonged to those six children that were just adopted by that lady you drove home." I says, "They weren't related, were they?" and she says, "Sure they was, they's all sisters and brothers." She knew because she had seen the papers that were filled out when they came in."

Letty turned to Chloe and Daniel. "Is this true?" Chloe nodded and Daniel hung his head. "But wait, wait. Did you said Walker children?"

Franklin grinned. "Yes, Miss Letty, let me introduce you to your great-nieces and nephews. This is Daniel Isaac Walker, age eleven. This is Chloe Elizabeth Walker, age twelve. Eveline Letitia Walker, age ten. Elijah Wade and Oliver Franklin Walker, age eight, and Grace Patience Walker, age six. They are the grandchildren of your broth-er, Elijah Walker, from Walker Mountain."

"Are you saying my babies and Elijah's grandbabies are...?" Letty gasped and gathered the children around her. Chloe and Daniel stood behind her with their arms around Letty's shoulders. The twins were in her arms, while Grace and Eveline sprawled across her lap.

"My, um, my brother?" She stared at Franklin.

"The same, my dear, the very same. There was an epidemic," Franklin said sadly. "I've been able to trace the family through their old neighborhood and talked to several of their old neighbors. They told me what they could but didn't know all the details."

"His son?" she asked hopefully.

"Their mother, Elizabeth, died in childbirth. Wade,

76

your nephew, left the children with a neighbor, Alton Cooper, while he looked for a job. He traveled with a friend down near Seven Springs and got a job in the coal mines and sent a letter to the Coopers, but the children had already went looking for him. Cooper tried to contact their father but was informed there was a cave-in and, well, he wasn't located.

"How the children got to Seven Springs is a story only they can tell you, but the end result is nothing short of heaven sent, I can tell you that. The conversation you overheard, your determination to take unknown children, and the unbelievable gift Miss Patience left you, is a miracle. That's all I can say."

"Children, why did you pretend you weren't related? Letty searched their faces.

Chloe stepped forward. "At first, everyone knew, then they forgot 'cause nobody really cared except for a few. Daniel and I noticed that families got separated quickly. I overheard a staff member say that brothers and sisters caused more problems than children that didn't have anyone. We wanted to stay together and, well, Daniel and I thought it was best to pretend that we didn't know one another."

"I guess it worked," Franklin said with a chuckle. "Here you are."

"Aunt Letty, I don't understand. What is everybody saying?" Grace fretted. "Why is he talking about Papa and Grandpapa? What is he saying?"

"I'm so sorry, darling. Mister McDougan has just brought us news that your daddy was my brother's son. I know that must sound confusing, but to put it simply, I really am your aunt. Your honest-to-goodness aunt and nobody can never, ever take you all away from me. You are my blood and your history started right here on this mountain. Your grandpa stood right where you're standing and slept where you sleep. Every trail you take, you're walking where he walked.

"I don't know why, or how, the good Lord did it, and I'm not one to question. I just know He brought you back home. He brought you to me, where your mama and papa and grandpa would want you to be."

"But your name is Wade and Papa's was Walker," Eveline said. "Why don't you have the same name like we all do?"

"I was a Walker when I was born. When I married, my name became Walker-Wade. I just use Wade because it is proper to takes you husband's name, but you always carry your born name in your heart. You'll understand one day, my dear."

"I'm never gonna change my name," Grace said. "And I'm gonna stay right here on this mountain forever. I don't want to change a thing."

"All changes aren't bad. But I hope you do stay nearby, my darling."

"I don't understand how you found us, Aunt Letty." Chloe shook her head, her face a mask of confusion.

"Remember what I told you all about hope? You didn't understand how I knew you were all alone and needed a home, remember? I don't have all the answers. I think I told Franklin that very same thing not long ago. But it isn't the answers that are important, nor is it the questions. It is the faith that we are required to have and faith brings hope and hope—" she stopped when Daniel interrupted.

"...makes all dreams possible," he completed her sentence with a wide smile.

~ Five ~
Lesson of History

"Just think Eli, our grandfather stood on this very hill and looked out across this very valley." Daniel put his arm around his little brother's shoulder and they gazed over a snow covered dale.

"I wonder what made him leave," Oliver said while walking up beside them. "Why would anyone want to leave a place like this? You could hunt and fish and explore forever and still never see all of it. Why didn't he just stay here?"

"The same thing that made us leave New York and go looking for Pa," Daniel told him. "We didn't want to stay there anymore. We wanted to go somewhere else."

"That wasn't the same at all," Eli said. "We needed Pa."

"Sure it was. First, it's the need to know what's over that next hill, and second, it's the hope to find a place where you can grow and become a better person."

"Couldn't he be a better person here?" Eli asked sadly. "Maybe he'd still be alive if he'd stayed here."

Daniel grinned. "And maybe we wouldn't have been born if he'd stayed here. After all, he wouldn't have found and married our grandmother, and he wouldn't have had our pa, and we wouldn't have been born to them like we were."

"Okay, I get it." Eli said. "But I wish we could have all grown up here and been a family with our ma and pa and grandparents," Oliver said. "Some families stay together all their lives in one place." Tears filled his eyes.

"And some don't. Look at what happened when the fever hit New York. Look at the families that were split up when the war tore them in two and some, thousands, never came back," Daniel tried to expand Oliver's thinking.

"But we would still have—" his brother started to argue.

"Oliver," Daniel snapped. "Look at where we were two months ago and look at where we are now. There's an old saying about not crying over spilt milk. That means there's no sense in whining or complaining about things that have already happened, or things you can't change or do anything about. Listen, you two, somehow, don't ask me how, our Aunt Letty found us in a world where we were lost and forgotten.

"Remember all the kids there? Do you think they found people who'll love them the way Aunt Letty loves us? No they won't. I think Mama and Papa were looking over us and, who knows, maybe they led Aunt Letty to find us, we'll never know. We do know, though, that we're together and have a good home with someone who'll care for us like our own Mama. Don't look back, Eli, Oliver, just look ahead." Daniel smiled and ruffled the twins' hair.

Oliver grinned and Eli nodded. "You're right, Dan. We're here now and that's what really matters. I think Mama and Papa are truly looking out for us, and Grandpa, too. We're sorry, Daniel, we'll be better." Oliver punched Eli playfully.

Back in the cabin, Franklin and Joseph were gathering up their coats, preparing to leave. No amount of Letty's coaxing could persuade them to stay. Joseph finally admitted his feelings about Daisy and was anxious to get back to Seven Springs and continue his efforts to court her. Franklin said his new wife had urged him to tell Letty the news about her family face-to-face, but he needed to get back now, tie up ends at work, so he could take time off to spend with his family during the holidays. He asked Letty what her plans were for Christmas.

"I just realized how close it is," she admitted. "I hadn't mentioned it until you and Joseph drove up shouting, *Merry Christmas*." She laughed and looked around. "As soon as they get over the shock of being a real family by blood, they're going to remember that and then I'll have to speed things up."

"You still have plenty of time for shopping," Franklin said, "unless you have a blizzard, then what'll you do?"

"You know, this money I inherited isn't going to change my life much," Letty mused slowly. "It's nice not to have to worry about feeding and clothing the children, but we're going to live like God intended us to. We're going to work hard, laugh a lot, and help others. These children are going to learn that money isn't the answer to their problems. Don't look so worried, Franklin. They're going to have a wonderful Christmas, I promise, but they're going to have it the old fashioned way. The way Christmas was celebrated when I was their age. I'll write you all about it after the holidays.

"And please, thank your new wife for her insistence that you tell me about the children in person. It means so much to me and be sure to wish her Merry Christmas from us. I hope I can meet her soon. After all, she's married to one of my best friends.

"Joseph, I wish you well with Daisy. I can see how much you care about her, and from what the children told me, she's a very warm and loving person. She'll be a wonderful wife for you and a loving mother for all your future children. I hope you win her hand. Please let us know how things work out."

Before Joseph could react, Letty stood on tiptoes and planted a quick kiss on his cheek. "I'll never forget your kindness, Joseph. Most people would have just thrown that box away and not have thought about what it's contents meant. You are a kind and thoughtful person and you'll be rewarded."

Joseph mumbled his thanks and shifted from one foot to another, smiling and blushing.

Franklin laughed and hugged Letty before starting for the door. Letty and the girls waved goodbye from the porch and saw the boys running alongside the carriage waving and shouting, "Merry Christmas."

"Oh, mercy." Letty smiled softly. "It's begun."

Letty reached up and began to rapidly ring the old dinner bell that had hung from the porch supports since she had been a child. The boys stopped and stared at the cabin. She rang it again and motioned for them to join her. They ran quickly to the porch, laughing and trying to be the first to arrive.

"We have some planning to do, my dears. As you have heard, Christmas isn't far off. Let's go in, have a cup of tea, and discuss what all we have to do," she said.

Chloe and Eveline prepared the tea, while the twins put the cups on the table, and Daniel replenished the cookies on the plate. Grace placed napkins all around and they all sat eagerly awaiting the discussion of the upcoming holiday.

"Chloe, how did you celebrate Christmas at the orphanage?" Letty asked. "What kind of food did you have?"

Chloe frowned. "It was no different than any other day for us," she said grumpily. "The staff always had a feast. We couldn't see it but we could smell it. You know, chicken and pies. They ate in the kitchen while we ate in the dining room."

Daniel spoke up. "We usually had cabbage soup, and on Christmas they gave us bread to eat with it. Chloe's right, though. We could smell chicken, ham and pies being baked in the kitchen. It made our mouths water."

"Sometimes, fancy ladies would bring cookies and cakes at the holidays for us but the matron took them all and never gave us any. They took them for themselves," Eli grumbled. They said we were gonna get 'em later, but we never saw those cookies again."

"Are we having cabbage soup?" Grace asked innocently.

"I'm sure some of the churches and ladies groups took holiday donations to the orphanage. Didn't you get any presents?" Letty asked, ignoring Grace's question about the soup.

Daniel snorted. "You don't have any idea, do you? Once, when one of the boys asked what happened to the gifts one of the ladies brought, the head matron hit him on the side of his head and asked what he thought we'd do with presents, and then, she just laughed. We never saw anything that people brought for us."

"Aunt Letty?" Grace repeated, tugging on Letty's skirt impatiently. "Are we having cabbage soup?"

"That's one of the things we're here to discuss. Would you like to have cabbage soup?" she teased.

They dropped their heads, but Chloe spoke up. "It wasn't too bad. We can have it if that's what you want, ma'am."

"I want roasted turkey with apple and raisin stuffing. I want baked sweet potatoes with toasted walnuts, green beans and sugared carrots. On the side I'd like some fresh baked bread and for desserts, I was thinking of pecan pie and apple torts with cider and cinnamon punch. We also can't forget to put out a plate for the fairies, so they will light the path to our cabin for Saint Nicholas." Letty had gotten some paper and was writing a list while she spoke. When she looked up, she saw six stunned, surprised faces.

"Oh, Aunt Letty, are we going to have all that?" Evelyn asked.

Grace tugged on Letty's skirt.

"I have most everything we need in the root cellar and the pantry. Daniel, would you like to go hunting with me one morning and bag us a big ol' turkey?" Letty asked.

"Yes, ma'am, I would, but I've never shot a gun," he admitted. "But I sure would like to try."

Grace crowded closer to Letty and tugged again on her skirt.

"I think we can arrange that. And we'll have to remedy the fact that you've never gone hunting," she said. "We have some time before the hunt. We'll do a little practicing in the next few days, we will.

"Aunt Letty, please," Grace cried.

"Oh, my dear, I'm sorry, what do you need?"

"You said something about the fairies lighting a path for Saint Nicholas. Are we having company for Christmas?"

Letty bit her lip. Reaching down she caressed the little girl's face. "You don't know who Saint Nicholas is?" When Grace shook her head, Letty pulled her onto her lap and motioned for the others to come near her.

"From what I was told, Saint Nicholas was a wonderful old man who loved good little children and wanted them to know the love of the Lord, who is good to everyone. After little children go to bed on Christmas Eve, he creeps from house to house and leaves wonderful surprises in stockings hung on the mantle for all children who have been obedient, caring, and good to man and creature alike."

"Oh." Grace stuck her thumb in her mouth and stared at Letty. Pulling it out quickly, she asked, "How does he know we're here and will he think we've been good?"

"My mama said he asks the fairies, the woodland creatures, and the elves who see everything, and they report to him who's been good and who's been naughty." Letty looked around, studying the faces of the children.

"What happens to those who haven't been good?" Eli leaned forward.

"I hear they get bags of rocks, sticks, and lumps of coal, while the good children get fruit, candy, and perhaps a pretty ribbon or a marble."

"I hope he thinks I'm good," Grace said. "I'm going to be extra good from now on."

"I seriously doubt he'll leave you sticks or stones in any of your stockings. You all have been extra good, at least, that's what I've seen and that's what Daisy told me. I'm sure the fairies have seen it, too. Now, let's get back to preparing our celebration.

"Chloe, you and the girls need to go out to the barn and you'll find a box in the last stall. In it there will be a large bag of pecans and walnuts. Bring 'em in and start cracking and shelling."

She checked several things off her list, then put the paper down and looked around at the smiling faces. "We have another thing to discuss. The choice of gifts."

"We don't need gifts, Aunt Letty. Just being here and having that wonderful dinner is gift enough," Daniel said with a smile.

Eli jabbed him hard in the ribs and turned his attention back to Letty. "What about those gifts, Aunt Letty?"

Letty smiled and began to write their names on small pieces of paper. "You will each choose a scrap of paper. Each piece has one of your names on it. Girls will draw first and boys will draw last. That way you can help each other with your gifts and the giver will remain a secret.

"Where will we get the gift, Aunt Letty?" Grace asked.

"Why, you'll make them, of course," Letty answered. "I will discuss the gift with each of you, advise you, and perhaps make a suggestion or two, and believe me, you will be able to make a wonderful gift. That's the way we did it when I was growing up. It was so much fun trying to hide our gifts from each other, trying to get them all finished in time."

Grace clapped her hands together. "That sounds like so much fun. I can hardly wait. Hurry, let's take a name."

Letty folded up the scraps of paper in small pieces. "Now, take a name but don't tell anybody whose name you drew. We'll make it a secret. They won't know until we exchange the gifts on Christmas morning. Won't that be fun?"

"That's wonderful," Eveline cooed. "Oh, what fun. Hurry, Aunt Letty, let us pick one. Can I be first?"

Letty placed them in her bonnet. "Now close your eyes, reach in, and pick one out. Don't show anyone. Hide

85

the paper and we'll each talk later about what to make."

She let Eveline go first and after that each child closed their eyes, stuck their hands in the bonnet, snatched a piece of paper, they ran off to peek at it.

Grace stayed at the table. "Aunt Letty, I forgot something. Will you help me with mine? I can't read."

"I couldn't either when I was your age. My ma had to tell me whose name I had. Bring it to me." She leaned back and reached for the paper. Letty peeked at the name, leaned over and whispered in Grace's ear. "You've got Chloe."

Grace clapped her hands. "Oh, goody, I've got—"

Letty clapped her hand over Grace's mouth. "Shh, remember, it's a secret from the person on the paper."

Grace grinned. "Oh, I forgot. I won't tell, I promise. This is such fun. What will I make?"

Letty put her fingers to her lips "Shh, don't you worry, little one, we'll talk about it later." Grace nodded and giggled while dancing around the room.

"All right, you all have a name now, so give it some thought. Daniel, put on your coat, I'd like to see you on the porch, please. There is something that I have to show you."

Daniel struggled into his coat, followed his aunt out, and trailed behind her until she reached the shed beside the barn. She walked in, leaving the door open for Daniel. He watched her carefully remove a large quilt that covered a sturdy chest. Pulling some keys from her pocket, she carefully unlocked the chest and opened the lid. Letty motioned for him to come join her.

"Daniel, this box of tools belonged to your great-grandfather, your grandfather, and now belongs to you and the twins. The twins are a little young but with your supervision, I'm sure you all will take good care of them and build something fine. There are saws, planes, gauges, sand blocks, hammers, and all sorts of thing-a-ma-jigs I don't know about. There are also tins of nails, screws and plugs. Over there, under some more covers, are pieces of cherry,

maple, walnut, and oak boards of all sizes, shapes and colors.

"There is a book of drawings in the bottom drawer of
that container. My grandpa and pa always drew pictures of
the gifts they wanted to make. None of them could read or
write but they were smart, nevertheless. Maybe you, Eli,
and Oliver can make something from all this. I know your
grandpa and great-grandpa would like that. Take your time
and look it all over. You can show the twins later. If you
want, I'll take a look and we can talk about what you want
to make.

"Here, you keep the key. It's yours and these tools
are yours, too now, and I trust you to keep them safe for
your children and their children. It's a grand responsibility
but I think you're up to it. In fact, I know you are. Like I
said, take your time, look through them, and come in when
you're finished."

Daniel touched the tools tenderly. "My grandpa's
and my great-grandpa's tools. I can hardly believe it. Thank
you, Aunt Letty. I'll take very good care of them," he said
softly.

"I know you will, Son."

When Letty went inside, she found the girls dancing
around in front of the fireplace, clapping their hands to
keep time. Eli strummed a make-believe banjo and Oliver
blew on an invisible harmonica. They were making sounds
with their mouths to mimic the music. Letty joined in the
clapping and soon they were laughing, and Grace got dizzy
from whirling around and around, and finally tumbled down
in the middle of the braided rug.

"That was wonderful, boys. You sounded like a regular musical band. Did you know your grandpa and his brother used to play the banjo? They performed for all the par-
ties." When they shook their heads, she continued. "When
we were young, some Saturday nights after the work was
done, Papa used to move the furniture back, roll up the

rugs and Ma would make apple cider with cinnamon for us. Some of the neighbors would come over, Elijah and Isaac played the banjo and ukulele, and your grandpa played the juice harp while we clapped.

"Ma and some neighbor ladies cooked all sorts of good eats. Then we ate and danced all night. Maybe next summer we can have a barn dance. Does that sound like fun?"

"Sure does," Eli said, laughing. "That sounds like a lotta fun but I didn't know barns could dance."

Letty laughed. "You are such a silly boy, Eli. The barn doesn't dance, you goose. We all dance in the barn."

"He knew that, Aunt Letty, didn't you?" Grace giggled. "Even I know that pigs don't fly and barns don't dance. That's a joke, get it?" She giggled again.

"Chloe, you get started on the biscuits for supper and I'll get some ham from the smokehouse. Eveline, can you get us some beets from the cellar? Ham with red-eye gravy, beets, corn, and biscuits sounds good to me. How about you young'uns?" Letty asked. She rose and smoothed her apron. They nodded and scattered to get busy while Letty headed outside to get the ham and drag Daniel away from the tools.

During supper, Letty announced that it had been a long time since the cabin had been decorated for Christmas, but things were about to change. "Tomorrow we will go out into the woods and gather some holly and pine limbs to drape around the porch frame and around the front door. My ma used to lay them across the mantle and tie colored ribbons on the limbs.

"You know something? We need to make a trip into town in the next few days to pick up some sugar and baking powder. I feel like making syrup cakes for the neighbors. It's been a long time since I've done that. Remind me, Grace, I need to pick up some needles, thread, and ribbons. Can you remember that?"

Grace nodded. "Can we go, Aunt Letty? Can we all go?"

"Certainly you can. It'll probably be the last trip to the store until early next spring. I've never gone this time of year. I hope it doesn't snow again until we get back. We need to get our supplies as soon as possible. Why don't we go tomorrow and then get the holly the next day?"

"Yay," Grace shouted. "Needles, thread, and ribbons. See, I 'membered. Needles, thread, and ribbons," she said in a sing-song voice.

Up before dawn, they dressed, ate, fed the chickens, and cleaned the kitchen before the sun rose. After hitching Tiny and Pokey to the wagon, they watched the sun rise over the road to town. They pulled into Kings Camp by eight o'clock and tied up the team just as the general store opened.

Floyd was so gracious and polite, Letty was tempted to tell him to relax. By the way he smiled, and hovered over them, Letty suspected Denton Parker, the banker, confided about the money that had been transferred to an account for her. Floyd had always been courteous, but today he outdid himself. Throwing *this* in free and telling the children there was no charge for *that*.

"I'll take nothing we don't pay for," Letty told him. "I will check the bill carefully before we leave just to make sure. Everything had better be listed, too. Do you understand, Floyed?" He eagerly agreed but she did see him slip the children little pieces of candy now and then.

She pulled him into a corner and handed him a list to be filled. "These things are to be wrapped securely and placed under the wagon seat while the children and I are shopping down the street. I don't want the children to see the purchases. I will be back to pay for everything before we leave," she assured him.

"And tell Mrs. Cramer to include about ten cans of milk in our order, plus two ten-pound sacks of sugar," she said to Chloe, who was looking at some watercolors and paper.

"But Aunt Letty, Sookie gives us over a gallon a day. What do we need canned milk for?" Chloe asked.

"For snow ice cream, my dear. It's truly delicious. Haven't you ever had snow cream?" she asked. When Chloe shook her head, Letty replied, "Then, you're in for a real treat, I assure you, a real treat."

After looking around a bit and talking to Floyd again, Letty clapped her hands loudly and called the children together. "Come children. While our order is being filled, I want to take you down the street and show you the different businesses. This is your town now, a place where you will grow up and I want you to know where everything is."

Once outside, Letty lowered her voice and whispered softly to them. "We need to go down to the bank for a minute. Mister Franklin gave me this paper to take to the banker. We have to sign a card so we can get money out if we need it. I don't see that we'll need it anytime soon, but in an emergency, we won't have time to think about that. I didn't want those nosey folks in the store to know where we are going. It's none of their business."

"And we don't want to get robbed," Grace added solemnly.

"Right," Eli added.

Denton Parker had always tipped his hat to Letty when he saw her, but today, he almost fell over his feet when she walked in.

Letty remembered how Franklin had grinned when he told her she needed to take the papers to the banker. He would have sent the papers by mail, he said, but he wanted Letty to see what affect money had on people and how it changed the way some behaved. He told her he knew that in a few months, she would be a great deal richer than Denton Parker would ever be, and Franklin laughed when described how Parker would probably try to convince

Letty to invest in some wild-haired notion. He warned her it would probably be some-get-rich-quick scheme that he had manufactured. Franklin assured Letty he knew she was no one to try to scam, and if she was anything like her Aunt Patience, she would jerk that bank right out from under Parker's feet if she found out he had cheated any of her neighbors or friends.

"Miss Letty Wade, how delighted I am to see you, just delighted. Please, come into my office and have a seat. What lovely children, indeed, lovely children. Mister McDougan informed me that you might be dropping in. I can't tell you what a pleasure it is to be of service to someone like you. Yes, a pleasure. I was thrilled to hear the stupendous news of your wonderful good luck, absolutely thrilled.

"Bernice, bring us a tray of tea and cookies, please. You will have a cup of tea, won't you, Miss Letty?"

The children stood agape at the manner in which the banker was fawning over their Aunt Letty. They didn't understand half the things he was saying or doing.

"Yes, tea would be nice, Mister Parker," Letty agreed.

"*Denton*, please call me Denton. After all, we've known each other nearly all our lives, haven't we? Yes, indeed, all our lives. We're old friends aren't we, dear lady? Yes, old friends. Children, did you know that your aunt and I are old friends here in Kings Camp?"

"Be that as it may, Mister Parker, I just wouldn't feel right calling you by your given name. You introduced yourself to Frank and me as Mister Parker when you turned us down for that loan my husband asked you for, remember? Frank wouldn't put the mountain land up for collateral and you said we didn't qualify since we had no assets of value to back up the loan. Do you remember that, *old friend*?" she asked, sarcastically.

"Miss Letty, you must be mistaken. There has been some misunderstanding. I don't remember Frank, or anything about collateral. I just can't recall," he sputtered.

"No, *Mister Parker,* I am not mistaken. There isn't any misunderstanding. One doesn't forget something like that. But, no matter, that's water under the bridge. I believe you have some papers for me to sign and I have some papers for you. If anything happens to me, I want these children to have the mine, should it be working or not. I want them to have the land that Aunt Patience left to me, and I want them to have all the money in the bank."

"Fine, fine," Parker said anxiously. "But Miss Letty, this account is adding up fast and I think you should consider investing it for the future. I have several excellent ventures that will double your money in a just a year. Time's a wastin' if you want to get on the bandwagon. There are a couple of investments that you need to look at right away. You've got to be quick if you want to get in on the best deal. If we wait, someone else might get interested and then we would be left out in the cold. Let me show you wh—"

"*Mister Parker,*" Letty said in a barely controlled voice. "Where are the papers I need to sign? Here are the papers to insure the children will inherit my assets. Mister Franklin McDougan will be the trustee in case they are still minors if I should die suddenly."

"Miss Letty, I would be happy to be executor of your will and—"

Letty held up her hand and shook her head. "We seem to have a communication problem, Mister Parker. Am I stuttering? Are your ears plugged up? Either I am not making myself clear, or you are just not listening to me. Either way, we need to get something straight right away. This minute. Right now. Perhaps I should drop a letter to Mister McDougan and have my account transferred to—"

"No, no, no, Miss Letty. That won't be necessary. Here, sign right there by the "X" or just make a mark and—"

"Mister Parker, I can read and write as well as you,

and if we were as close friends as you say, you would have known that," she replied coldly. "You're among several people I've talked to lately who thinks that knowing someone gives them the right to call them a close friend, especially if they don't know the slightest thing about them or their abilities."

"Please forgive me, I spoke without thinking. Of course you can write. I should have known that. Here are the papers designating your children as heirs to your assets.

"Oh, thank heavens, here's our tea." He anxiously jumped up, his teeth grimaced in a strained smile.

"No, thank you, *Mister* Parker, I've changed my mind. I don't care for any tea and I have just lost my appetite. Come, children, I'm sure Floyd has our order filled. We must be on our way before the snow starts," she said, rising and smoothing her skirt.

Flustered, Norton Parker danced from behind his desk and rushed to open the door to his office. "If there is anything, anything at all that you need, or I can do for you, please, please, don't hesitate in calling on me. I am at your disposal anytime, day or night, during the week or on the weekends. And if you hear about an investment you are interested in, I'll be happy to check it out for you. Miss Letty, I want nothing more than for you to rely on me..." His groveling was cut short when Letty snorted and walked away.

She paused at the doorway. "By the way, Mister Parker, the name is *Mrs. Wade* to you, sir."

By the time they reached the general store, the wagon was loaded and Floyd waited just inside for them, looking anxiously out the window for their arrival. Letty carefully checked the receipt and when satisfied, she opened a small snap purse and counted out the correct amount. When she turned to leave, Chloe stepped forward.

"Aunt Letty, would you please go with Daniel and wait in the wagon for us. Mister McDougan gave us a penny each before he left and I want to help Grace pick something out."

"I don't mind waiting a few minutes, dear, go a-head."

"Please, go with Daniel, Aunt Letty. Grace wants to feel all grown up and buy it herself," Chloe pleaded.

"All right, dear, but don't take too long. We don't want to be caught in the storm. If we leave soon there won't be a worry, so spend your penny, but don't dawdle."

"Yes, ma'am, we'll hurry," Chloe said and grinned.

"I don't think it's gonna snow for a while, Miss Letty," Floyd remarked, looking out the window, up at the sky.

"You've lived on this mountain for a spell now, Floyd. You need to learn to watch for the signs. They're everywhere. The caterpillars are fuzzier this year, there haven't been any late calves born in the past few weeks, and nearly all the squirrels have gathered all they need. Even the last gaggle of geese flew south a couple of weeks ago. Signs, Floyd, you need to watch for the signs.

"My old friend, the hawk and my barn guest, the owl, started nesting indoors the week the children arrived. I guarantee you, it's gonna snow and it's gonna snow long and hard. Mind my words, Floyd, you won't have customer one tomorrow, unless it's Barney and Digger come in for a checker game and to drink your free coffee there, by the wood stove. Stay home tomorrow, Floyd. I'll see you come spring thaw, if the good Lord's willing and the creek don't rise," she said and laughed.

~ Six ~
# A Feather in Their Cap

Chloe, Letty, and the girls took all the packages inside and each one had special places for certain packages. Daniel and the twins unharnessed the team after backing the wagon into the shed. Eli and Oliver placed Pokey and Tiny in their stalls, brushed them tenderly, threw a warm blanket over their backs, and provided them each with a scoop of oats and a flake of hay. Daniel made sure the doors and windows were tightly shut and packed hay along the bottom of the back door and along the window sills of the barn. Deer skins hung on a rod inside the barn door that could be pulled across on cold, windy days and nights to help keep the wind from getting inside each time they entered the barn.

The boys walked toward the house and Oliver looked up and cried, "Look, Daniel, look. Aunt Letty was right."

When Daniel looked up, he saw a few tiny crystal flakes float lazily down like thistles in the meadow in the springtime. However, the longer they stood and watched the flakes drift down, the heavier and fluffier they became. Within a few minutes it was as if a sheet drifted over them. Large, thick, fuzzy clumps of snow sifted down faster and faster. Even as they stood there, visibility grew fainter.

"Run, y'all, run." Eli shoved the boys forward and raced for the house. They saw Letty coming from the chicken house and knew she had been pulling down the prop-up windows, securing them and the doors, and making sure the hay was piled up against the north wall. She stuffed some extra hay in the laying boxes for the hens to snuggle down in to lay and made sure no snow could drift in through the roof of their warm little house.

They all ran laughing up onto the porch and shook off the snow before going inside. They stared a while long-

95

er from the window, watching the yard and road become covered with a white, silvery blanket.

"Ready for cocoa, ham, and biscuits?" Chloe smiled and stirred a fragrant pot of hot chocolate. Eveline and Grace set the table and in addition to the cocoa, Chloe prepared a pot of coffee for Letty.

Letty and the boys nodded eagerly, scraped their boots off, and hurried inside as the temperature quickly dropped.

Letty sat, inhaled the welcome cup of coffee, and asked, "Did we get everything we needed? If not, we'll just have to make do. I expect the mountain trail to be completely iced over and covered in snow until spring. We do have some neighbors in case of emergency, but they need their supplies as badly as we do. I've always made do, but then," she paused and chuckled, "I never had anyone else to worry about."

"I think we got everything," Chloe answered.

"What neighbors?" Grace piped up. "I thought we were all alone up here. I didn't see any other houses nearby."

"No, little Grace, we're not all alone. The reason you didn't see any houses is that up here, folks don't build their houses very close together like they do in the city. Everyone up here likes their privacy and they need their fields and gardens nearby for tending. They're good people and you can trust them with your lives, but they don't visit too often in this weather. In fact, you don't see them much in the spring or summer.

"They will come to barn dances, and will help get in crops or replace damaged houses or barns, but mostly they just keep to themselves. In the spring, they plant their crops, in the summer they tend to them and hunt to fill their smokehouses. In the fall, they can and dry fruit and vegetable, dry skins, and in the winter, they trap, and stay inside to keep warm.

"The Patterson's live northeast of here about six or

seven miles. They have eight children, but they're a lot older than all of you. There may be a few more young'uns by now. The Wilson's live about five miles west of here, and they have twin girls about ten years old, and a boy around eight, and two older boys close to seventeen or so. They all stay very busy helping around the farm, so you won't see much of them until school begins. Not every child around here attends school since they're needed at home and school is quite a piece away. I'm hoping to remedy that in the near future."

"School?" Will we go to school?" Eveline asked excitedly.

"Of course you'll go to school. Every child in this family goes to school. Some of them didn't go long, but they went. I was the only one in my family to graduate and I wouldn't have then if it hadn't been for my Frank. He finished school and taught me. I was barely fifteen when I married, and when I took the graduation test at seventeen, my whole family was there. It was the first and only time I ever saw tears in my pa's eyes. He may have cried at other times, but no one ever saw it.

"No one can cheat you if you can read and write, he always said, and I've found over the years that what he said is the truth and something to always remember. I taught him to read a little and write some. He was so proud the first time he wrote his name. I had tears that time."

"When do we go?" Grace asked.

"You're too little. You can't go," Oliver teased.

"Can too," she insisted.

"Can't," he argued.

"Children, I don't even know when your birthdays are. Grace, I'll bet Miss Biddle, the school marm, will let you go if you sit still, listen, and try hard. She's a very sweet lady and all the children are very fond of her. I'll have to teach Daniel and Chloe to drive the team."

"We were talking about the neighbors," Chloe reminded Letty.

"Oh, yes, well, like I was saying, you'll probably meet them at school after the spring thaw. No one up here on the mountain can travel the road to school until after the thaw," Letty told them. "Now drink your cocoa before it gets cold and let's get the kitchen cleaned up. Don't you all have some thinking, deciding, and planning to do?" Letty tilted her head and smiled.

They all nodded and finished their snack. The boys cleared the table and the girls washed and dried the dishes. Letty had been the only girl and remembered how unfair she thought it was when her brothers never had to help in the house. Her brothers had been assigned to the outdoor jobs and caring for the animals. They plowed, cut and baled hay, planted the garden, and chopped the wood. She wouldn't have minded outside chores and she grew so tired of housework. She and her mother weeded and watered the garden but the housework was boring and seemed to never get done. When the children arrived, Letty decided every one of them would share all the work, indoors and out. So far, it seemed to be working well. The girls and the boys seemed happy with the arrangement, and there hadn't been any complaints from either.

Each child seemed to be lost within their thoughts tonight and Letty suspected they were thinking about the gift they were to give or perhaps the gift they would receive. Whichever, it was a pleasant sight as Chloe wiped off the table and Daniel dried out the washing tub. The twins were stretched out on the floor in front of the fire, while Eveline and Grace whispered together in the corner.

Letty worked on a needlepoint she started months ago and felt a gentle touch on her shoulder. When she looked up she saw Chloe smiling at her.

Daniel scooped up Eli, who had fallen asleep on the floor. He mouthed goodnight and carried Eli upstairs. Oliver yawned, got up slowly and trailed sleepily after Daniel.

"I just wanted to thank you for everything you've

done, and are doing for us. I lay awake at night sometimes and wonder what would have happened to us if you hadn't come. I can't imagine what kind of work they would have made baby Grace do. Eli and Oliver, too. They're so little and aren't very strong and I..." she choked up and Letty reached out and gathered her close.

"Sit down, Chloe, and I'll tell you a story. Not a make believe story, but a true one and you must listen with an open mind. It may sound strange, but it really happened.

"Shortly before I got the letter about Aunt Patience passing, I started having dreams. They were dreams about six little flowers in a field and all around them, the woods and meadows were dying and they were all alone and soon, they too, would be swallowed up by the nothingness. I had it the night I arrived in Seven Springs, only that night, a hawk told me I had to help those flowers.

"The next day I overheard some of the guests at Chastity's house talking about an orphanage closing and that there were six children left with no place to go except the work house. You children were the flowers and your future was the nothingness that surrounded you in my dream.

"I think someone special told me to go get you. Your grandpa sent the hawk in my dream to tell me. Your grandpa and his brother thought hawks were the most wondrous birds. He must have shared his feelings with your papa and perhaps he told your mama. Maybe she sent me. I'm not sure. We have one living in the attic, you know?"

"One what? A hawk? A real live hawk?" Chloe stared, her mouth open, her eyes wide.

"Yes, he's been rooming there for some time now. He seems to know he's safe here with me, and now with us."

"Aunt Letty, do you think that hawk is watching over this family for grandpa?"

Letty's eyes grew misty at the thought. "My dear

child, at this moment, I'm not sure what I think. All I know is we're all together and that's the way it's supposed to be, regardless of the how and why. The good Lord works in mysterious ways.

"Now, you must get to bed. We have to start preparing for the holidays tomorrow. It's been so long since I've had a real Christmas, I've forgotten what all we need to do. I'm gonna have to make a remembrance list."

"It's been a long time for us, too," Chloe said. "But together we can figure it out, I'll bet." She kissed Letty firmly on the cheek and hugged her tightly.

The first kiss Letty had in many a year. Tears formed and she watched Chloe climb the stairs. Everyone needed someone to love and someone to love them back. The children had an overabundance of love to give and they also needed it so badly.

She rose, went to her writing desk, pulled out a paper, and began to write. The preparation of Christmases long past flooded her mind. She remembered all the wonderful decorations and holiday foods her mother and grandmother used to fix. They had given their family the very best they could afford and spent hours of love preparing everything. She wanted the same for her new family, her six little flowers, and she wasn't going to miss a thing, not one single thing. She didn't bother asking them their favorite food. It had been so long since they had eaten regularly, they probably wouldn't even remember what they liked or didn't like. Right now, they liked everything. So far, the only thing she had discovered that none of them were too fond of was liver. They had eaten it, but she had seen the look on their faces and made a mental note not to fix it again.

The next morning Letty prepared breakfast, Chloe and the girls gathered eggs, fed the chickens, broke the ice on the water trough, and checked the fence around the chicken pen. Daniel and the twins checked on the horses, milked the cow, fed them grain, and made sure they had water and hay.

Once inside, Eveline discovered one of her mittens was missing and ran back to the chicken coop to find it.

Letty was scrambling eggs when Eveline's screams cut through the quiet winter morning like a hot knife through butter. Daniel jumped to his feet and started for the door.

"Wait." Letty snatched the gun from above the mantle. She grabbed her shawl, slung it over her shoulders, and jerked the door open while pulling back the double hammers of the shotgun.

Eveline's screams were muffled and she crouched down against the chicken coop with both hands covering her face.

Standing in the lightly falling snow outside the fence was a strange apparition. Covered from head to toe in layer after layer of assorted furs, feathers, and beads was a fierce looking figure. His hat was fashioned from the furs of a fox, and rode low on the stranger's forehead. His fur boots came up to his thighs and were crisscrossed from ankle to knee with strips of rawhide. A coyote tail covered the man's nose and mouth leaving only his wide eyes visible. In one hand, he carried an old musket and in the other, a long spear decorated with shells, beads and feathers that he used as a staff to test the snow depth. He stood unmoving, staring at Eveline.

Daniel skirted around the fearful sight and ran to grab Eveline while Letty grinned and lowered her gun. Evie continued to sob and sniffle while Daniel led her to stand behind Letty.

"Evie. Aunt's Letty's here. Evie, hush. Eveline." Daniel shook her hard until she lowered her hands, hiccupped, and sniffed.

"Eveline, Daniel, this is Cherokee George. He's perfectly harmless, at least harmless to us. He's a friend of mine. He lives on Pecan Ridge over there." Letty pointed across the nearby hills to a peak beyond the forest.

Evie continued to hide her face and gulped. "Daniel, take Eveline inside and clean her up. George, come into the kitchen with me. You must be freezing. How's your family? Well, I hope."

The fur clad figure nodded and followed Letty into the house, leaving his gun and spear leaning against the wall outside the front porch door.

Chloe and Grace watched from the window and Chloe grabbed Eveline the moment Daniel brought her through the door. She took off her coat and hat, and examined the tearful child thoroughly from head to foot and even checked her hair.

"Did he hurt you, Eveline? Did he hurt you?" She grabbed her sister and turned her around, staring into her eyes.

Eveline shook her head and grabbed Chloe around the waist. Still trembling, Chloe held her tightly, comforting her sister with a gentle pat.

The door opened and Letty and George entered. Eveline looked up, howled, and buried her face in Chloe's shoulder. All the children backed up behind the table.

"George, take all those hides off and let them see you're just a man. I never thought much about the way you dress, but I must admit you are a sight." She slapped his arm playfully and chuckled.

The big man's shoulder's shook slightly and a short laugh bubbled from his muffled face. He swung a large bundle from over his shoulder and let it hit the floor with a loud thump. The children jumped, but stood fast. He pulled off his deerskin gloves, unfastened his coat, uncoiled the furs from his face, reached up and removed the fox-head hat. Two long, dark braids decorated with feathers and beads fell over his shoulders. His sky-blue eyes sparkled with glee.

"Top o' the morning to ya, Miss Letty, and thanks for rescuing me from that tiny banshee," he said with a heavy Irish brogue. "I thought fer sure I was done fer. Never heard such a mournful cry. I wouldn't be surprised if she woke up every sleepin' critter from here to yonder and back. She would be wondrous for long distance talking, wouldn't ye, my screamin' lil gal?"

"Chloe, pour our visitor a cup of coffee. Eveline, you and Grace put another plate on the table. Children, gather around. Daniel, I didn't have time to get the jam. Could you get it for us?" Letty led George to the end of the table, sat next to him.

None of the children spoke. Evie's sobbing had disappeared but she still clung to Chloe's skirt. She would only sit Chloe between her and the strange, scary visitor with the blue eyes and funny sounding speech. She was curious but still very nervous.

George slurped his coffee eagerly. His cup was empty before anyone else had taken a sip of theirs. Letty refilled his cup, passed the eggs, ham and biscuits around and finally had a chance to sip from her cup. George began to cram the food in his mouth, chewing loudly, grunting his approval and nodding.

"George, what brings you out in this weather? I figured you'd be holed up for the rest of the winter. You aren't still running traps, are you? I would think you'd be checking them rather than exhausting yourself traipsing around the mountain in all this snow."

"Already finished tha traps fer this trip. Why sure, and it's your shining self that brings me out today. I was in town about a week ago, with my last batch of furs, when Floyd tells me you showed up in town with a wagon full of wee babes. I told him he were daft, but no, several others couldn't wait ta tell me it were true, and what's this rumor about having a bank full of money? They ain't sure you got any, but they're talkin'."

"Don't rob us, Mister. We don't have no gold," Eli

whined, squirming on the bench.

"Rob you? Why bless your heart, my wee laddie. I'm here to give you somethin', not to rob you. What have you been telling 'em, Letty?" He threw back his head and laughed loudly.

"If you're an Indian, how come you talk so funny?" Eveline asked, beginning to warm up to this strange man.

"Sure and did you ever hear of an Indian being born in Waterford, Ireland? No? Well, that's where I was born, lil darlins'. Ireland, God's green jewel on this earth." George smiled, stood, and did a little jig.

"Then, why do you look like that?" Daniel asked.

George looked at Letty, who nodded, and then looked back at each face of the enraptured children. "Da an' I came to the mountain when I was just about thatn's age," he said, pointing to Daniel. "We got here just before the pass closed an' that winter was one of the worst that ever was. Da wasn't very knowing, he was still grieving over the loss of me ma. He went out to check traps one day and hasn't been seen since.

"Several days later a huntin' party came across our camp. I was nearly frozen and half-starved when they found me. They took me to their camp, they did, and raised me like one of their own. They looked for me Da but decided that he had fallen into a deep crevasse or had been buried in an avalanche. They gave me a good home, treated me like a son, and here I am. The end. Not a very excitin' story, but then I'm not a very excitin' fellow, just a plain and ordinary son of the Emerald Isle."

"Why don't you speak Indian?" Oliver asked.

"Oh, I do, laddie, but I like to speak me own tongue whenever I gets the chance. Fate is a tricky fellow, he is. There was an old Irish priest near the Indian camp. He took it upon himself to keep me close to my own past by teaching me Irish history, legends, and me own language, which I could hardly understand. He spoke mostly Celtic, but we made out, we did. When I was in the camp, I had to learn their language or starve. I'm jokin', they wuz as kind a people as there ever wuz. In time, they wuz like me own family, and I could hardly remember not livin' with 'em."

Eli shyly waved his hand. "You said something about not robbing us but bringing us something?"

"That I did, me boy, that I did. Floyd was tryin' to tell me about the young'uns, but his recollection wasn't too clear to me. It being close to Christmas, I thought I'd stop by before the blizzard hits, and it will, Miss Letty, it will. This here is only a little snowfall. The one that's comin' in the back door is a doozy, trust me." He pointed to a pack by the door. "That one there is yours."

George drained his cup, rose, and clomped across the floor to his pack. He carefully untied the thin leather straps around the bundle, folded the covering back, and laid several fur items around on the floor.

"Now, although I trapped these magnificent foxes and praised them for their sacrifice, I'll have to admit, I didn't make these items. Running Doe, my Cherokee sister, fashioned them for me. I told her there were six little new-comers to the mountain and I wanted them to have a wel-come gift for Christmas. She thought these hats would be warm and I agree. She worked very hard on them, she did. Come, little ones, I think you'll like them."

With their fear gone, the children scrambled from the table, snatching up the soft reddish-golden hats. Grace slipped hers on first and cooed, "Oh, it's so soft. It's just beautiful. Thank you, Mister Cherokee. I love it."

Chloe and Eveline rubbed their faces against the silky hats. "Please tell Miss Doe that they're the most won-derful gift we've ever had," Chloe said softly.

Daniel and the twins slipped theirs on and wrapped the long fur tails over their shoulders. "It really is warm," Daniel said.

"Do I look like an Indian, Mister Cherokee, do I?" Oliver asked, bending over and moving his feet in a little dance.

"Indeed you do, lad, indeed you do," he said with a chuckle. "And I'd appreciate it if you'd just call me George, everybody does, don't they, Miss Letty?"

"Yes, children, you may call him George. Now, let's not waste this food. Please, come back and finish your breakfast," Letty said.

"One final thing," George announced and delicately peeled back the deerskin folds of another package, this one much smaller.

"This is from my Indian father, Stalking Wolf. This is a great honor for you." He picked up six magnificent feathers and went to each child, securing the feathers in their hats. "These feathers are from the hawk, his spirit walker, who guides him in the path of life. He hopes they will always guide your feet to safe paths and happy places."

"Oh, boy," Eli said. He grabbed Oliver's shirt and pulled him near the mirror to admire their reflection.

"Please tell Stalking Wolf and Running Deer that we are honored by his wonderful gifts. Thank you, George, for the beautiful furs," Letty said softly.

"I'll tell them, Letty, and you're most welcome for the furs. Now, let's get back to that breakfast, what do you say, me wee bairns?"

After breakfast was finished and everything was washed and put away, George began to dress for his departure.

"George, you know you're welcome to stay a few days, don't you?" Letty said.

"I know, me dear lady, but I want to get home before the blizzard. I don't want to end up like poor ol' Da. Besides, I have some store-bought presents for my family. I want to surprise them." He grinned and motioned toward his pack. "My sister loves pretty ribbons, and my father is hooked on that sweet pipe tobacco Floyd carries." He chuckled and continued to dress for his departure.

"About that blizzard?" Letty asked worriedly.

"Oh, don't you worry, Letty. You and yours are safe

enough if you string rope from the house to the barn and chicken coup ta guide you back and forth. You just don't want to go anywhere else.

"Our medicine man said the animals told him the blizzard would start tomorrow and last five days. Your place here is in no danger from avalanches. So, as long you stay put or only use the ropes to the barn to check on the chickens and livestock, you should be fine. I know you've got enough food for six months, don't you?" Without waiting for an answer, he jammed on his hat and crammed his hands into his mittens.

"I'll see you after the thaw," he said cheerfully. "Mind your Aunt Letty and stay inside," George warned the children. "Welcome to the mountain. See you later," he shouted, opened the door, grabbed his gun and spear, and trotted across the yard.

He stopped, turned and shouted, "Letty, don't open the other package until after the blizzard is over, ya hear?" He started trotting again and with a final wave over his shoulder, soon was out of sight.

They huddled together on the porch and watched George disappear over the far hill before they turned and went back into the warm house.

Letty stood staring at the fire for a full minute and then turned to the children.

"We need a little extra preparation. I expected the snow, but I didn't realize it would be last so long. George is so good about coming around and telling us all.

"First, let's make some snow ice cream. We'll just take some snow, add some vanilla, sugar and canned milk. It's delicious."

They watched Letty make the ice cream and couldn't believe how wonderful it tasted. They ate until their little bellies were bursting.

"Now, let's go over the last minute things we need to do before the blizzard hits. Are you all ready to work a little?" She asked.

The children moaned, rubbed their stomachs and nodded.

~ Seven ~
Mountain Christmas

*A*fter thinking about the oncoming storm, Letty told Daniel and the twins to throw extra hay for the livestock and put a another small bale in the hen house. Chloe filled a long tray of feed for the chickens and reinforced the windows and the doors.

Letty put on a big pot of venison stew, then she and Eveline got the ingredients for bread. If she was going to have the fire going for the next few days, it might as well be put to good use. After the regular bread was baking, they mixed up some with extra sugar, raisins and dried fruit. Letty worked on her syrup cakes to deliver after the blizzard. While the girls were baking, the boys went to the shed for a secret project and stayed until almost supper. They brought in several strange looking, covered bundles and quickly hid them in their rooms. After supper, the children excused themselves and disappeared upstairs, leaving Letty to relax and await the blizzard.

The medicine man's prediction was right on the money. Shortly after dawn the next day, the skies darkened, the snow fell heavier and the winds picked up. Daniel and boys gave the livestock extra rations and divided a bale of hay for the horses and cow. They filled the water troughs to the brim. The day before, Letty had checked the barn and doubled the cover of skins over the open window. She left several small chunks of bacon, ham and venison for her resident owl. She did the same in the attic for the hawk. Neither were frightened or nervous by her presence.

The wind whistled and moaned all day and the children helped Letty bake cookies, and later spent the afternoon in their rooms working on their secret gifts.

Four days later, the wind died down, the snow ceased falling and the sky brightened a little. Daniel and the twins had checked daily on the livestock and tried to keep a trail cleared to the house.

During the final night of the blizzard, snow had banked up against the house and the only way they could see out was to climb on a chair and look out the top of the window. As Eli jumped down, his foot struck the package that George had left Letty.

"Aunt Letty, here's your package from Cherokee George. Did you forget about it?"

"Yes, dear, I did forget about it," she answered.

"Open it. He said for you to open it after the snow stopped, didn't he?" Eli jumped up and down in his excitement.

"All right, don't have a fit. Here, let me see." She smiled and began to untie the rawhide straps George had secured around the gift.

The children gathered around and peered anxiously over her shoulder. When she pulled the last fold back, Daniel let out a yell. "Snowshoes, everyone. George left us all snowshoes. Yippee, now we can go outside and see about the chickens and horses, and check on the cow. They've been locked up a long time."

"Just hold your horses," Letty said. "Daniel, go upstairs, put on your snowshoes, climb out the upstairs window, scoot along the roof, and work your way to the barn so you can check the livestock.

"Light the wood stove in there and make sure there's no hay nearby so we don't have to worry about burning the barn down. Break up the ice in the water troughs, if you can, and put some water in buckets in the stalls after you feed. Make sure they have plenty of hay and give them a couple of handfuls of grain.

"Then, you can check the softness of the snow on the way back to the house. You'll have to shovel the doorway clear so we can get outside. Do you think you can do that or do you want Chloe to help you?"

"Chloe?" Daniel snorted. "Chloe'll slide off the roof

and break her neck. She could never shovel all that snow. Don't worry, Aunt Letty, I'll have all that done in no time. It's not as deep near the door as it is around the windows. The boys and I shoveled it every day. You kids go ahead and eat, I'll have mine when I finish." He puffed out his chest and began to put on his warm clothes to get ready for his chores.

Daniel fed the livestock, heated up the barn, melted snow for not only the livestock, but the chickens as well. He gave the horses some grain and hand-fed the cows a little, too and threw some grain inside the chicken coop, and the chickens attacked it hungrily. He carefully started shoveling pathway clear back to the house. After taking the shovel back to the barn and securing the barn door, he went back to the house and knock loudly. "Aunt Letty, come see. I finished and we can all come out now."

Letty opened the door and dragged Daniel inside. "Boy, what took you so long? I was about to send a search party out looking for you."

Daniel ducked his head and explained. "I figured the chickens needed some feed and water, too. I let the barn warm up and the horses and cows are fine. I wanted to shovel enough so you wouldn't have any trouble climbing out. Sorry I worried you, but I wanted to do a good job, so you'd be proud of me."

"Daniel, I am proud of you, but I don't want to find you frozen stiff. Son, many an experienced mountain man has misjudged his endurance and been found sitting against a tree, or curled up without a breath left in his body. I don't want that for you."

"Yes, ma'am." He gasped as she crushed him to her.

"Okay, now peel out of those clothes and sit down and have some breakfast. I know you must be hungry."

"Aunt Letty?" Grace said smugly. "If it's so dangerous outside, why did Daniel have to clear the doorway? Why don't we just stay inside?"

"We have to care for the animals and the chickens,

you know. They provide us with transportation, milk, butter, and eggs. They're good to us and we owe them good
food and warm shelter. Don't you agree?" Letty asked looking over her spectacles at Grace. "Especially when they
need our help."

"Yes'm," said Grace miserably. "I'm sorry. I never
thought about it that way. They're as much our family as
we are, aren't they. I'll never forget that again."

While Daniel wolfed down his breakfast, Letty pulled
Grace into her lap. "Grace, you've had to worry about you
and your brothers and sister for far too long. There's been
no one you could depend on. That's all changed now.

"You can depend on those chickens outside to lay
eggs nearly every day. You can count on Sookie to provide
milk for you to drink. From Sookie's milk we get butter for
our biscuits and to season up the vegetables. And you can
depend on me, my darling, to love you and take care of
you, Chloe, Eveline, Daniel, Eli and Oliver. Now, since you
have so many others working hard to care for you, you can
think about all the nice things you can do for them. How
does that sound?"

"I like that." Grace grinned. "I like that a lot.
Aunt Letty, can we make presents for the animals for
Christmas?"

"I suppose so," she chuckled. "But, only after you've
finished the gift for the person whose name you drew. Okay?"

"Okay," she agreed.

"When you've finished eating, Daniel, the girls will
clean off the table and after we wash the dishes, we'll all
go out and find some decorations for the house. We'll have
the most colorfully decorated house on the mountain."

The rest of the day was spent gathering cedar, pine,
and holly branches. After the girls and Letty cleared the
snow from the porch, the children piled it with the branches, then leaned over the rails to shake the snow from the

greenery. Letty stared across the clearing for a moment or two and then squared her shoulders.

"Come, it's time you met your family. We'll come back after the thaw and stay longer, but a quick hello won't do any harm. Bundle up, strap on your snowshoes and follow me."

The children gave each other a puzzled look, but obeyed their aunt and followed her obediently across the yard through a small stand of trees and up a small nearby hill.

The snow was knee deep, but there were rounded humps protruding. Here and there a tall cross stood proudly. Letty knelt down and began to brush the loose snow away from one of the bumps in the snow. Deeper and deeper she dug. Daniel and Chloe helped her and soon the lump was revealed to be a tombstone.

Irene Rosella Morgan Walker was the name roughly carved in the stone. "This is my grandmother, your great-great-grandmother. On that side is her husband Abner. Next to her is Martha Anne Walker, my ma and Harmon is next to her. We won't dig any more. I just wanted to introduce you to them. That cross there was Aunt Patience's mother-in-law and beside her lays her father-in-law. They were born down over there at Lightning Gap. Her husband, God rest his soul, is the man who won our gold mine during a game of poker. I don't know if he was shot during that game or not, but at least he didn't gamble the mine away.

"Over here is your great-uncle Frank, my late husband. Lord, how he loved children. I'll bet he made cradles and rocking horses for half the children on the mountain. I know he did for every child born in this family.

"Children, there's not a doubt in my mind that your Uncle Frank is smiling down on you this very minute.

"This spring we'll come back and pull weeds and plant some flowers. We'll pretty it up real special. That way you'll enjoy coming up and visiting with them now and then. There's something special written about them on each stone. It's called an *epitaph*. You can learn a lot about them by reading their epitaphs, a little history and sometimes a little about the person."

Chloe slid up beside Letty and slipped her arm around her aunt's waist. "We'll take good care of the cemetery, Aunt Letty, I promise," she said softly.

"We sure will," Grace added. "They're our family."

Daniel stood apart from the rest, looking out over the lower meadow below. "I never want to leave here," he said firmly. "This is where we belong. I feel it in my heart."

"There may come a day, honey, when you won't feel that way," Letty said sadly. "But if you do leave, you'll know you'll always have a home to come back to."

"No," he said dreamily. "Others may leave, but I won't. Not ever. I know what's out there and this is where I want to be. I'm never leaving."

"Me neither," the other children chorused.

Letty smiled and closed her eyes. She knew they felt that way now and that was good, but later, well, she'd just have to deal with later, much later.

"Don't y'all have a gift to be working on?" she said with a chuckle. "We'll shake out the boughs and hang them up on the porch to dry off. Tomorrow we'll tie them around the rails and over the door and fireplace."

~ * ~

The cabin was quiet except for the sound of Letty lifting the lid of the pot occasionally to taste the venison stew. The girls were in their rooms busy with their gifts, and the boys were in the shed working on theirs.

Letty sat in the big rocking chair by the fire, reading her Bible. Suddenly, she sat up straight and shouted, "Daniel, Daniel, come down. Children, you all must come down. Hurry, times a'wasting."

The children came bounding down the stairs, wide-eyed and anxious. Letty had her coat on and motioned for them to do the same. Bewildered, the children quickly

114

donned their coats, hats and gloves, and slipped into their boots. They had to run to catch up with Aunt Letty as she hurried out the door.

"Wait there," she told them, and hurried toward the barn.

Soon she was back carrying the big ax across her shoulder. She jerked her head sideways in a gesture to follow her, turned, and marched around toward the back of the cabin and disappeared into the woods. The children scampered to catch up with her.

"Aunt Letty, what's wrong? Where are you going?" Daniel called, working his legs side to side to make it easier for the others to follow.

"We have to get a Christmas tree," Letty shouted over her shoulder. "It's a little over two weeks until Christmas and we haven't got a tree. We have to cut it, build a stand for it, make paper chains, string popcorn, find berries, and there're gum balls to paint. If we want to decorate properly, we have to get busy. No time to dawdle. Keep your eyes peeled for a pretty shaped tree. Not too tall and make sure it's full and healthy. Don't want all the greenery to die and fall on the floor."

"A Christmas tree?" Grace screamed and giggled.

"Oh boy, a Christmas tree," Eli and Oliver said in unison.

The children spread out and began to examine every tree. "Here's one," Daniel yelled.

"No, this one's perfect," Oliver hollered.

"I like this one," Eveline called out.

"This one. This one," Grace insisted, doing a little dance around a scrawny tree.

"Here. Come look at this one and tell me what you think," Letty said.

When they had all gathered around Letty, they stared at the tree she selected. It was about six feet tall and four feet wide at the bottom. It tapered gently upward to a point and was thick and full.

"Oh, my," Eveline whispered in awe while Grace just sighed and stared in wonder at the beautiful tree.

"It's too big for the door," Oliver said softly.

"It's the most beautifulest tree in the whole wide world," Grace gasped. "Can we have this one, Aunt Letty?"

"Only if," Letty said, looking around at the beaming faces, "you all agree on this one. Otherwise, we can just keep looking."

"I vote on this one," Grace said loudly.

"Me, too," Eveline agreed.

"It's the best," Chloe said with a nod.

"We say *yes*," Eli and Oliver said in a duet.

"I don't think there is a better one," Daniel said, approvingly. "Aunt Letty, may I cut it down?"

"Absolutely," Letty said softly. "Children, move back, let's not get in Daniel's way."

It wasn't as easy as Daniel thought, but eventually it fell. Letty pulled out a rope from beneath her coat, fastened it securely around the base and told them all to grab hold and they would pull it home.

At the cabin, they shook off all the snow and Letty took the saw to cut off the bottom squarely. Daniel and the twins located some wood scraps and fashioned a base for it with Letty's supervision. They dragged it inside, where Chloe and the girls cleared a corner for it and set it up after Letty placed a pan of water under the freshly cut end.

For several minutes the children just sat and stared at it in silent admiration. Letty felt her eyes burn with tears as she wondered how long it had been since they had seen a real Christmas tree. She couldn't wait until they saw it decorated up with brightly colored paper cut-outs, chains, ribbons, berries and popcorn.

Letty went to her room, brought out a package and sat it on the table. She cut the twine that held it and let the wrappings fall open, revealing colored paper and ribbons.

"O-oh, look," Grace cooed and they all gathered

around.

"Grace, here's my scissors. Eveline, will you help her please, so she doesn't cut herself? Now, you two cut the ribbons into small enough pieces to tie into bows on the ends of each limb. Daniel, here's another pair of scissors for you to cut little shapes like stars, circles, squares and triangles, while Eveline punches holes near the edge. Eli, you and Olive take this string and run it through the holes in the shapes and make it long enough they can be tied on, too. Grace, why don't you let Eveline cut the ribbon by herself? I need you to help me pop some popcorn and we'll string it into long ropes tonight and drape the ropes around and around the tree. Daniel, make sure you save a large enough piece of paper so we can cut a big star out for the top of the tree to remind us of the one over Bethlehem. Let's get busy."

The rest of the day was spent cutting, tying on ribbons, designing colorful cut-outs, and popping corn.

Eveline concentrated on carefully punching holes in the paper shapes with one point of a baking fork so they could be hung, and Eli and Oliver cut small lengths of string and ran them through the holes.

Letty popped the corn and Grace spread it out to cool on long flat pans and separated the small pieces to be eaten and the large pieces to be strung.

After a cold supper of ham, cornbread, spiced tomatoes and hot tea, they strung the popcorn on thread and draped it on the tree from top to bottom. Letty also showed them how to take little strips of paper and make a circle and glue it together with a paste made from a little flour and water. They slid each strip into the circle, glued it and repeated the process over and over until a long multicolored chain was the result. It, too, was draped around the tree. When the last chain was placed around the top, Daniel lifted Grace so she could top the tree with the yellow star. He sat her down and they quietly gathered together.

They all sat on the floor around the tree, stared and smiled. Grace reached out and touched one of the apple shapes Daniel had cut out. "Pretty," she said and smiled at him. "They're so very pretty.

"Thanks." He grinned.

"It's all so lovely," murmured Eveline.

"Yeah," chimed in Eli and Oliver. "We did good."

"Well," Letty corrected. "Indeed, you did well."

The clock on the mantle chimed ten o'clock.

"Mercy," Letty cried. "Look at the time. I'm exhausted, aren't you? Let's pick up all the scraps and put them back in the brown paper. We'll find a box tomorrow and maybe we can use them later. Now, we must go to bed. I'm too old to be staying up this late," she said and laughed. "But it was fun. In fact, the most fun I've had in ages."

The next couple of days flew by. The children would rise early, do their chores, and disappeared into their rooms. They would come down for lunch, eat, clean up and were gone again. They would appear whenever Letty called them, do her bidding, and then went back to their rooms.

At night, after supper, Letty read them a story. Lately, it had been from the New Testament leading up to the Christ Child's birth. Grace gazed at the tree during the story and before they went up to bed, the children all paused to admire the tree, touch it tenderly, and scurry up to their rooms.

Early one chilly morning, Letty woke Daniel up before dawn. "Daniel, get up and get dressed. We have to get the turkey today. I have to clean it, let it cure, and prepare it for Christmas dinner. We have to get it today. Get up."

Daniel leaped out of bed and hurriedly dressed. When he crept downstairs, he saw Chloe and Letty at the stove. "Drink some tea, child, and eat some biscuits and bacon. We'll leave before the little ones wake up, and if we're lucky, we'll be back in a couple of hours. I heard a turkey or two last week when I was out in the yard. I believe we'll get one if we get out to the meadow early this morning.

"Chloe's going to be in charge of things till we get back. Make sure the children get all their chores done before they start working on their gifts. I know they are anxious to work on them, but after all, work comes first. At least, the care of the animals do."

"Don't worry, Aunt Letty, I won't have to remind them. They really love the animals, even more since you've been reading the story of the coming of Baby Jesus. Grace has even been asking if we could get a donkey like Mary has in the story when she and Joseph travel to Bethlehem."

"There's even more animals in the manger where Joseph and Mary spend the night once they reach Bethlehem. Tell her that and she can have even more to look forward to," Letty said softly.

After a quick breakfast, Letty and Daniel dressed warmly, and slipped on their snowshoes. They left tracks across the yard as they plodded past the cemetery and walked down into the valley and hid down in a clump of bushes. Letty pulled a small carved reed from her pocket and began to blow little bursts of a strange rattling sound.

Nothing but silence surrounded them. Again, she blew into the reed, silence. They waited for about half an hour with Letty blowing now and then, but no turkey. She put her finger to her lips and slowly rose, motioning for Daniel to follow her quietly. They walked across the field and through the brush into a small clearing.

They repeated the calling and waiting and just as they started again into a different area, a sound, ever so slight caught Letty's attention. Squatting down, she motioned for Daniel to bend down also. She blew on the reed and the call echoed across the field, nothing. She repeated the warble again, and this time Daniel heard an answering garble from across the meadow in a small stand of trees. Letty blew it the fourth time and Daniel shook her arm and pointed. From the trees and underbrush, a large, shiny black bird, spreading a fan-like array of black and white feathers and a long swaying waddle under his neck came strutting into the meadow. Daniel started to rise, but Letty pulled him back down.

"Shh," she cautioned. "Wait."

The turkey gobbled and poked his head around trying to locate the sound heard. Letty answered with the reed and slowly cocked the two hammers on the shotgun. Without rising, she carefully took aim and waited. The Tom turkey gobbled again and walked proudly closer.

Letty looked down the barrel, held her breath, aimed, and pulled the trigger. A roar filled the air and scattered a covey of quail from nearby underbrush. The discharge from Letty's gun knocked her backward and Daniel threw his hands over his ears. Letty scrambled to her feet and started running. Daniel, his ears still ringing, followed.

Letty started laughing and hollered back, "We got 'im, Daniel, we got 'im."

Letty reached the turkey, grabbed him by his feet and held him high in the air. Daniel grinned when he reached her and took the bird from her hand. It was so heavy he had to use both arms to hold it up off the ground.

"This spring, after I teach you how to handle old Betsy, here, you'll be bringing in birds, deer, elk and maybe a wild boar or two."

Daniel nodded eagerly, took her arm, and they started back to the cabin. "I thought it would take us all day," he said.

"Sometimes it does and sometimes we're lucky, like today," she said.

When they reached the cabin, Chloe had a large black pot of boiling water bubbling on the stove. Letty had told her that they would need the hot water if they were lucky enough to get a turkey. She had to dip the turkey in hot water to make plucking the feathers out easier. Letty chopped off the turkey's head, slit it up the middle and pulled out the innards, and then began to pull off the outer feathers.

She took it inside and dunked it in the boiling water, then picked the feather quills from its skin. It took most of the morning to prepare the turkey. When it was clean and fairly smooth, Letty rubbed it down with salt and pepper, and hung it outside on the back porch to stay cold.

Each day, one child or the other would ask, "What day is it, Aunt Letty?" or "How much longer, Aunt Letty?" to which she answered, "Not long, now dears, not long." Finally, one morning, she announced, "You have three days left to finish your gift, today and tomorrow, and the next day. Tomorrow is the day before Christmas Eve and the next morning is Christmas Day Eve. The day after is the day of Christ's birthday, Christmas day and that's the day we exchange gifts and have our wonderful feast."

At that, they rushed upstairs, giggling and laughing. Letty continued to chop, mix and stir things together. Each time she put something on the cold storage porch, she thought of Frank. He added the storage porch the first year they were married. They had talked of the big family din- ners they were going to have with his family and hers, and decided the cold porch would be necessary to store all the food so they could start cooking several days before Christ- mas. He also laughed and told her that someday they would have lots of children, and one day, the house would be overflowing with grandchildren whooping and laughing. She could feel his presence with each pie she baked, and each cake she frosted. There was also a twinge of sadness that he wasn't here to see all the children in the house. She hoped he was looking down on them.

Every day the children worked on their gifts or snuck out to the storage porch to *ooh* and *aah* over the cookies, pies, and cakes that were collecting on the porches.

Chloe helped mix the dough for some of the cookies and pie shells, while Eveline and Grace had been allowed to help mix the ingredients for the cookies and pies. They also helped Letty mix the cakes and frost them. Letty insisted on baking the syrup cakes herself. She said she would teach them how later, but it was faster to do this herself since there was no written recipe. It was a pinch of this and a dab of that, and she was afraid her pinch and dab wasn't the same size theirs would be. She laughed when she told them because that's exactly what her mother had told her when she was a little girl.

They finished supper one night and after washing dishes and cleaning up the kitchen, the children gathered around the tree and began to talk softly to one another. They didn't run upstairs as they usually did. They were relaxed and extremely pleased with themselves.

"I take it you have all finished your gifts?" Letty asked with a smile, working steadily on her needlepoint.

"Yes, ma'am, we have. We finished 'em up, wrapped 'em, and now all we have to do is wait. We've never had such a wonderful time as we have in getting ready for this Christmas. I know you don't want us to thank you but we just don't what else to say," Chloe said softly, kneeling by Letty's chair.

"I know how you feel. I felt the same way when I was a girl this time of year, but you know, I'm having as good a time as you are. If any thanks are to be given, it's to the Good Lord for bringing us all together. Tomorrow is Christmas Eve and we'll get all the last minute things together and I'll finish up the story from the Bible. Then, day after tomorrow is the grandest day of all. Just wait, if you think you've had a good time up to now, just wait." She chuckled and caressed Chloe's cheek.

"Can you read some to us now?" Grace begged. "Maybe just a little while?"

"I'd like nothing more," Letty said. She put up her sewing and picked up the Bible. After reading up to the part where Mary and Joseph entered Bethlehem, she closed the Bible and looked at the droopy eyed children.

"Time for bed, little ones. Tomorrow is a busy day. Give Aunt Letty a kiss and get some sleep."

After everyone was in bed and the last lamp extinguished, the hawk ruffled his feathers, squawked once softly, and tucked his head under his wing.

Before dawn, Letty rose, chopped up the vegetables for the casseroles, peeled the potatoes and punched down the dough that had risen overnight for cinnamon rolls. She dropped a cut-up chicken in a pot of boiling, seasoned water and moved it back so that it could simmer.

She crumbled up cornbread, added onions, sage, and the shredded dry heels of old bread. She sprinkled salt and pepper and set it out on the porch. She also chopped up apples, added raisins and walnuts, and seasoned vinegar to them. Tomorrow she would mix it all up with eggs and chicken broth and stuff it in the turkey, and fill the pan with the dressing that wouldn't fit inside the bird.

Letty formed the sweet rolls and slid them in the oven and mixed up a pot of hot chocolate for the children's breakfast.

It wasn't long before the children came downstairs slowly, each one carrying a carefully wrapped gift they placed gently under the tree. Their faces were covered in smiles while they munched on cinnamon buns and sipped hot cocoa. Letty hummed a hymn while she cleaned up the kitchen and after their meal, the children went outside to make sure the greenery still hung over the porch rails.

After doing their chores, Letty told them the story of Saint Nicholas. Frank's brother had married a young girl from Norway who had told them the way they had celebrated Christmas in her country, and Letty had loved the story of St. Nicolas.

She laughed when she reminded them of the story

she told them of the gifts he brought good children and the stick, stones, and chunks of coal he brought those children who had been bad and mischievous.

Grace threw her hands over her face and said, "Aunt Letty, I feel so sorry for bad children."

Chloe said, "You need to feel proud for the children that have been good and maybe the sticks and stones will make the bad children be good the following year."

They sang Christmas carols, told stories but the day passed slowly. They played guessing games and Grace finally fell sleep around two in the afternoon simply from the excitement of the day. Daniel and the twins practiced their alphabet and Chloe read aloud to Eveline as she wound a skein of yarn for Aunt Letty. After supper, the children went to bed early with hopes that sleep would come quickly and Christmas morning would soon arrive.

Letty knew that the anticipation would leave them sleepless and edgy. She dozed in her rocking chair and jerked awaked when a log snapped in two in the fireplace. She tiptoed upstairs and looked in on the children. She could tell they had tossed and turned long before sleep came by the way their covers were twisted and the way their arms and legs were sticking out from under the quilts. She recalled how hard it had been for her as a child trying to go to sleep when she knew what awaited the very next day.

After tucking in all the arms and legs and snuggling the covers up under their chins, Letty snuck quietly downstairs and slipped into her room. Slowly, with aching joints, she knelt down on the floor and pulled several packages from under her bed. She placed them on the top and sat beside them, then unwrapped each one, while listening for footsteps on the stairs. She rewrapped each item and carefully tied each one with twine, labeling them with all six names. After several trips into the living room, she placed the assorted packages under the tree and stood back to admire the decorations.

She hadn't felt this good in so many years, she couldn't remember the last time. Even all the aches and pains from pushing her body further than it had been in many a year, Letty felt young and invigorated. Giving was a blessing, and she felt so blessed she thought her heart would burst. Her brother's grandchildren. She hoped he was looking down smiling that crooked smile of his and saying, "Good job, Baby Girl," his pet name for her.

Closing her eyes, she saw the faces of Frank, Elijah, and Isaac in her mind's eye. She remembered the early days when they wrestled, jostled, and fought to be the first one to open their presents. They made everyone laugh; good memories of good days. That was one of the times when she was happiest, and now, she was happy again.

She folded up the paper that Floyd had wrapped the parcels in and stored it away. She changed into her gown, kissed Frank's picture, said her prayers, and fell into bed. The clock chimed three o'clock when she finally dozed off.

~ Eight ~
The Family's First Christmas

"He came. He came. Aunt Letty, Saint Nicolas came!" The cries jolted Letty straight up in bed. She felt as if she had just closed her eyes.

A tiny fist beating excitedly on the door, brought Letty to her feet. "I'm coming, children, I'm coming." She struggled into her robe, working her feet into her slippers.

When she pulled the door opened and stumbled out, she expected the floor of the living room to be covered in brown wrapping paper with string and ribbon scattered across the floor. Instead, she saw six stunned children standing in awe, holding onto each other, and staring under the tree.

She hurried into the room and quickly looked in the direction they were staring, expecting a bear, or at least a mountain lion to be the source of their wonder.

"What?" She asked, seeing nothing but the tree and gifts.

"Don't you see them?" Oliver whispered and pointed at the base of the tree where Letty had placed the gifts the previous night.

"See what?" Letty asked as she scanned the corner carefully. "What in the world are you looking at?" she asked slyly. "Did a raccoon get in, or is there a mouse in the house?" She pretended to peer in search of it.

Eveline inched next to her. "Don't you see the packages there?" she asked timidly. "They're not ours."

Letty felt the tears burn her eyes and she pinched her lips together. "No, they're not. I guess you were either very, very good or there's several bags of coal wrapped up there." She smiled secretively.

"Oh, my," Grace said breathlessly. She crossed both hands over her mouth and her eyes grew big as saucers. Then she crossed two fingers and shut her eyes.

126

"Daniel, I think it might be better if you and Chloe picked out the gifts you all made each other. We'll check on the other packages afterward." Letty nonchalantly walked to the fireplace, laid several logs across the andiron, and stirred up the banked coals.

"I'll put on the water for tea and we can have warmed over biscuits and jam. How does that sound?"

The children continued to stand, unmoving, in front of the tree. Daniel slowly turned and looked at Letty. There were tears in his eyes and he said softly, "Grace, you and the twins find the gifts you made. Chloe, you and Eveline find yours next, and then I'll get mine. Just hold on to them until we all have one."

The little ones dove under the tree, grabbed the gifts they'd made, and scooted back. Chloe and Eveline picked theirs and then Daniel chose his. They stood quietly and watched for Letty to finish in the kitchen.

Letty returned from the stove and sat in her rocking chair. "Fine. Now, let's start with Grace. Whose name did you pick?"

Grace stood, still glancing under the tree and said loudly, "I picked Chloe's name. Chloe, Aunt Letty helped me with this but I picked out the colors and helped a lot." She handed Chloe her gift and sat down on the floor by Letty.

Chloe slowly opened the package and smiled. "Oh, Grace, it's wonderful," she exclaimed. It was a long woven scarf of multicolored strips of cloth. "How did you ever make this? I love it. I will wear it with everything."

Grace grinned and explained, "Aunt Letty has this board with lots of nails in it and you cut long strips of cloth, tie them together and wrap them up and down around those nails and then," she took a deep breath, "then, you weave some more strips in and out across those other strips and then, oh, I'll just show you later." She laughed and clapped her hands together in happiness.

"Oliver, you go next," Letty urged.

"I got Daniel's name and Aunt Letty showed me how to make, well, here," he said and shoved his present toward Daniel.

"Thanks," Daniel mumbled and unwrapped his gift. It was a foot long board with a "u" cut out in one end and a block of wood fastened under the cut end. It had been stained a dark brown and polished to a soft glow.

"It's a booter," Oliver explained. "You put your foot on the low end and stick your other heel in that cut out place and pull off your boot."

Daniel smiled. "This is great, Oliver. I've never seen anything like it. I didn't even know there was such a thing. Thanks a lot. You did a swell job." He turned it all around, admiring the workmanship.

"Eli, your turn," Grace squealed excitedly.

"I got Oliver's name and well, Aunt Letty said her brother had one and so I, so here, Oliver." He grinned and handed his gift to his twin.

Oliver tore the paper off quickly and his mouth dropped open. "Wow, a slingshot. A real slingshot and little round stones. Eli, this is just what I wanted, or would have if I had known you could make one," he said. "Thanks, brother, I'll let you use it, you know."

"I know," Eli said with a grin.

"Eveline, let's get back to the girls," Letty said.

"I got Grace's name and I knew that she liked to help Aunt Letty, so..."

"Eveline," Letty interrupted. "Let her open it before you tell her what it is."

"Oh, sorry." Eveline blushed. "Here, Grace, hope you like it."

Grace untied the string and folded back the paper. "O-oh," she gasped. "It's an apron just like Aunt Letty's. A little apron that really fits and look, it's got little flowers embroidered on it. Thank you, Evie, I just love it."

Eveline grinned, nodded and looked around.

"Daniel, I think it must be your turn. I believe you're

the last of the boys to give your gift," Letty told him.

"Eli knows by now I got his name, so here." Daniel slid the package toward Eli.

Eli grinned. "Thanks, Daniel, whatever it is, I know I'll like it. I've seen you working on it for a long time." He carefully pulled the paper off his package and his eyes grew wide.

"A boat! It's a boat with sails," he exclaimed. "How? Daniel, this is great. How did you ever..." he paused, at a loss for words.

"It's waterproof, too," Daniel told him. "Aunt Letty melted a candle and we brushed the wax all over the hull, the deck and the sails. She said if you take care of it, it'll sail for years."

"I will take care of it, I promise." Eli hugged it to his chest, his grin seeming to get wider than his face.

"Chloe, you're the last one," Letty said.

"Yes, and like Eli, I'm sure Eveline has figured out that I got her name. "Here, Sister, I made it especially for you," Chloe said softly.

"I'm sure you did." The little girl smiled and pulled the string from around the parcel.

"Oh, Chloe, a book, you made me a book. How'd you ever do it?" Eveline cried. "Look at the pictures and you sewed the pages together and look at the cover, and—"

"I told Aunt Letty what I wanted to make you and she showed me an old book she had when she was little. It was just what I had in mind. I looked at it very carefully and just made it like hers. She helped me sew all the pages together. Do you really like it?" she asked anxiously.

"Oh, Chloe, I love it. I've never had a new, never-been-read-before book. This is my very first book, ever. I'll take really good care of it, and when I have a little girl, I'll give it to her and tell her that her Aunt Chloe made it."

They all took turns examining each other's gifts, until Grace finally cried out, "What about the others? Can we look at those? Maybe we've been really good and if we have—"

"Wait," Chloe said loudly, "we still have—"

"Chloe, can't we wait until the end to, uh, you know? Daniel asked softly, tilting his head coaxingly.

Chloe smiled at Daniel. "Good idea. Aunt Letty, can we look at the other gifts now?"

"I'm sure they weren't meant to just sit there all wrapped up. You better see who they belong to and what they are. I'll bet they have names on them. Go ahead and see." She rose and placed a covered tin over the grate on the stove and put some jars of jam of the table. She also poured some milk in a pan and got the cocoa down.

"Why don't you just gather the gifts that have your name on it and put it beside you. When they are all divided, you can open them all at once," Letty suggested and waited for the milk to heat.

They all nodded and dove under the tree. Letty began to mix the hot chocolate, and to butter the biscuits with cinnamon butter.

"We have them, Aunt Letty," Grace called out, her face beaming. "Can we open them now?"

"Okay, I'll count to three. Are you ready?" She grinned.

When they nodded, she began to count, "One. Two. Three. Go!" And they began to tear into the gifts.

Letty placed the cups and saucers on the table, poured the cocoa, and set sweet rolls on the plates. The rattling of the paper suddenly stopped and there was dead silence in the room. Letty quickly turned around and saw the children quietly staring at the gifts around them.

Grace cradled a doll tightly to her chest with one hand, and clutched two little doll dresses in her other. Eveline also had a doll pressed against her cheek and she, too, had extra dresses for it.

Chloe held a sketch pad in one hand and a box of colored pencils in the other. There was also a tin of watercolors and brushes. Her lips were stretched into a wide smile.

Eli stroked a banjo, while Oliver looked at his harmonica. Both had music books in their laps, and a bag of
marbles. Letty had given Eli a slingshot, too, so now they
could both learn to use it to kill rabbits for stew.

Daniel stared at a .22 rifle and a box of ammunition,
along with large paper targets to practice on. He also had a
sheath for his gun and a cleaning kit.

All received readers, slate boards, chalk, pens and
tablets that were now strewn across the floor. A small China tea set lay beside Eveline and a doll cradle set beside
Grace. Two small bows with arrows were between the
twins and a spinning top sat in Daniel's lap.

"Aunt Letty, we don't know what to say. I, I..." Chloe
stuttered.

"That's right," Grace piped up. "How in the world
did Saint Nicholas know we were here? He never could find
us when we lived in Seven Springs."

"The world's a very big place and sometimes he
needs all the help he can get. I asked Mister McDougan to
drop him a note at the post office and tell him you were
here." She smiled and added, "I'm sure he was very sorry
he had missed you before. Maybe he was just trying to
make up for those Christmases when he couldn't find you.

"I'm gonna send him a letter and tell him he did just
fine and that it's alright that he missed us before. I just
hope he finds the other children that left," she said softly.
"Eveline, will you write it for me?"

Eveline nodded and hugged her sister tightly. It was
just like Grace to think of the other children on this special
day.

"Aunt Letty, can we go out and try our slingshots,
and boat, and rifle and, well, just everything?" Eli spoke so
quickly, it was almost impossible to understand him.

"Let's have something to eat first, get dressed, and
then go out and play. You children fold up the paper wrappings very carefully, and neatly roll all that twine into a

ball. We can use that over again sometime, I'm sure. 'Waste not, want not,' my granny used to say," Letty replied.

"Wait," Chloe cried. "Aren't we forgetting something?" She looked at the children sternly.

"Oh, yes," Eveline said.

"I forgot. I'm so sorry," Grace said, ducking her head.

"What are you all talking about?" Letty asked. "What did you forget?" She looked around the room.

Daniel got down on his hands and knees and reached far back behind the tree. He pulled out a package and the children gathered behind him. "Aunt Letty, this is for you, from all of us," he said and handed Letty the package.

Letty took the package and sat. Her hands trembled. "Where? How?" She looked at six pairs of eyes.

"Remember the money Mister Franklin gave us when he was here? It was more than just a penny. We took that and added the candy money you gave us when we were in town and bought you this. Mrs. Cramer at the general store said she thought you'd like it. We asked her if she thought it was a proper gift and she said it was truly proper and she would like it if someone gave it to her," Chloe answered quickly.

Letty folded the paper back and revealed a soft gray hat with tiny blue feathers, velvet leaves, and delicate berries on the side. When she picked it up, she noticed there was something hidden beneath. She moved a thin paper aside and there was a new shawl of soft, gray wool. A shiny blue satin ribbon was woven around the edge and tiny tassels hung from every corner. It was the same gray as the hat, and the blue ribbon matched the feathers. Her fingers moved gently over the shawl and hat.

"Oh, my dears, I've never ever had anything this grand. You shouldn't have spent all your money on me, but I will say this is the most beautiful hat and shawl I've ever seen. I'll be so proud wearing this. Thank you, my dear, sweet children, thank you." Letty picked up her apron and wiped her eyes.

"If she likes it, why is she crying?" Oliver asked, sounding confused.

"Girls are just like that," Eli explained. "Sometimes they cry when they're sad, and sometimes they cry when they're happy. You just never know unless you pay careful attention. I've been paying close attention and I think this is a happy cry, don't you?"

Oliver shrugged. "I guess," he said. "Girls are strange sometimes, aren't they?"

Eli nodded and picked up the paper while Daniel and Chloe began to fold it. Eveline, Grace and Oliver ran around, scooped up all the string and placed the twine on the table. Eli began rolling the string up into a ball. It didn't take long until everything was picked up and Letty put the paper and twine in a chest in her room.

The children quickly inhaled their food and drained their cups. After asking to be excused, they raced upstairs, dressed, and ran back downstairs to prepare to go out, do their chores, and play with their new gifts.

"I'll help with dinner, Aunt Letty," Chloe insisted.

"Me, too," Grace said, and turned her back to Chloe to have her new apron tied.

"Grace, why don't you and Eveline get your dollies all dressed for dinner and set up your little tea set for them. I think Aunt Letty has dinner almost ready and I just need to help her get the turkey in the oven. Saint Nicolas will think you don't like what he brought. You can help set the table later, okay?" Chloe said softly.

"We're ready, Aunt Letty," Oliver called as he and the boys headed toward the door.

"Children, one thing, please," Letty said quietly. "Today is Christmas and it's a day of peace and prayer in honor of the Holy birth just like what we read in my Bible. You may practice with your gun and slingshots out back in the woods but do not aim at any of God's creatures. Let

133

them have this day of peace and harmony, free from fear. Enjoy yourselves, but let nature enjoy itself, too. Remember, we do not kill anything that does not threaten us, unless we need it for food."

"Don't worry, Aunt Letty," Daniel answered. "We've never killed anything and we don't intent to hurt anything today. We probably couldn't hit anything if we wanted to, but we don't. We just want to go out and play and knock some leaves off the trees."

The rest of the day went smoothly. The boys slung rocks at leaves, limbs, and a few empty cans Letty provided them. Eveline and Grace set up a tea party, dressed and undressed their dolls several times, while Chloe helped Aunt Letty stuff the turkey and put it in the oven. The sweet potato casserole was placed on a rack in the fireplace and several pots of vegetables sat around on the stove to cook. The pies, cookies and apple cake were brought in from the storage porch to warm up, and a metal pot filled with apple cider laced with cinnamon and spices scented the room with a delicious aroma.

Around two o'clock Letty stepped out on the porch and rang the dinner bell. Across the yard, she saw the boys walking to the cabin talking to their fur clad friend, Cherokee George, who dragged something behind him.

"Welcome, George, Merry Christmas. What a surprise. Just in time for dinner," Letty called out.

"Hope you got plenty. I came around Morgan's lookout and saw a coach heading this way. Looks like you got more company than just me," he said with a grin.

"Can't imagine who it might be," Letty answered. "Not on Christmas Day. What do you have there?"

"Oh, I almost forgot I had this thing. My father's sister asked me to see if your young'uns would like to have this sled. Her boys have outgrown it, or at least they think they have, and all the other boys in the village have one.

"Daniel, do you think you and your brothers could

find a use for this old thing?" he asked.

"Oh, boy. Thanks, George. Please thank your aunt, too. Maybe we can do something for them one day," Daniel said gratefully.

"I know you want to go try out the sled, but if we've got someone coming, you need to get in and get cleaned up," Letty urged. "Come on, hurry in. Come on in, George. I have coffee on and you look frozen."

The boys came inside and cleaned up after hanging up their coats, scarves and hats, and took their boots to the back porch. The girls moved their dolls and tea party over to the corner and helped Chloe set the table. Letty and George chatted about some of George's family, while the children sat uneasily awaiting the mystery guest.

"Aunt Letty, why is it taking so long for the carriage to arrive?" Grace asked grumpily.

"The road is icy and covered in snow. It winds like a snake to get up the mountain. George's trail is high and across the tops of the hills, so he made it much quicker. It won't be long, honey," Letty answered.

Shortly, they all heard the sound of horses pulling up in front of the cabin. The children ran to the windows and turned to Letty. "It's Joseph, Aunt Letty. He's driving the carriage. There's some men inside, but it doesn't look like Mister McDougan."

Letty had a strange feeling. She put her hand against her chest. Her heart beat rapidly and her stomach did a quick flip-flop.

"Letty? Are you all right?" George asked, sounding worried.

"I'm fine, really, I'm fine. It's just, well, it's just a feeling. Granny used to have these feelings. I'm not sure if it's a bad omen or a good one. It's just—" she stopped when there was a knock on the door.

"You want me to get that?" George asked, looking at Letty with concern.

"No, it's for me. I know that much. It's for me and,"

she looked at the children who stood silently watching her, "and them."

Letty took a deep breath and forced herself forward. She grasped the latch and lifted it upward, then pulled it slowly toward her. When the door was fully opened, she saw an old man standing slumped-shouldered with his hat in his hand. He raised his eyes when he realized the door was open and asked nervously, "Letty, is that you?"

"Yes, I'm Letty Wade. Do I know you?" she asked. Her mouth went dry and her eyes itched. Her heart pounded so hard she was sure everyone could hear it. There was something so familiar about him, but it couldn't be, it just couldn't be.

Tears ran slowly down his deeply lined face. "I didn't think I'd changed that much, Baby Girl."

Letty screamed and covered her face, and in the next moment, she threw herself at the man and wrapped her arms around him. They held each other and cried openly.

"Elijah! Elijah! They told me you were dead," she sobbed. The old man hugged her tightly and the children crept around the door to stare at the strange sight.

"Did she say Elijah?" Chloe whispered to Daniel. He nodded, never taking his eyes off the crying pair. "Isn't he our grandpa?" she asked. Daniel shrugged and continued to stare.

"Look," Grace said and pointed toward the carriage. Joseph climbed down and helped someone down the coach steps. The man was bundled up in a hooded cloak and walked slowly, leaning heavily on a cane. Joseph held him on one side for support while they slowly hobbled along.

"Elijah?" Letty gasped when she saw Joseph and the other passenger. "Who in the world is that?"

The children stepped onto the porch with George close behind. They peered at the crippled man, and then he raised his head for a moment and glanced at the children.

Suddenly, Daniel yelled, "Papa!" He raced toward the two men and grabbed the man around his waist. Joseph struggled for a moment to keep them from falling to the ground.

"Papa," the children screamed and scrambled after Daniel. Soon Joseph and his passenger were engulfed with children hugging their father while they all cried.

~ Nine ~
The Long Trip Back Home

George rushed out to help Joseph get everyone inside the house. Letty had taken Elijah's arm and brought him inside.

"Oh, my," Elijah remarked, inhaling deeply. "I haven't smelled anything like that since I left home." He turned and quickly went to his son. "Letty, this is Wade Walker, my son, your nephew. Wade, this is my little sister, Letty, the one I told you all about," Elijah said to the younger man, and then helped him to a chair.

"I don't understand any of this," Letty said with a bewildered look on her face.

"I can understand that," Elijah replied. "I'm not sure I understand how everything happened either. I was living in a boarding house after my wife died, that is, me and Isaac were. Wade was living south of town with his family and had just been laid off from the packing plant.

"The fever hit fast and hard, and before I knew it, everybody on our whole side of town was either in the hospital or sick in bed. My landlady, bless her soul, took the sick right off the street and made them beds on the floor.

"I shared my room with Isaac and four others. Folks started dying right and left. Men would come in, wrap 'em in sheets, label 'em, and just cart 'em off. It happened so fast. I'd given Isaac my bed and I was on the floor beside him. I was so sick, I didn't know what was going on.

"Our dear Isaac didn't make it. He died, and they just got the name wrong. Those of us who made it, got back on our feet and tried to get in touch with our families. By that time, Wade's wife had passed and he had gone off looking for work, and no one knew where the young'uns were. I spent months looking, asking, going from job to job, hoping our paths would cross, but nothing.

"Then a young feller came into town and heard I'd

138

been looking for the fellow he'd left town with. It was Isaac's friend. He told me he heard that Wade had found a job near Seven Springs but was missing after a cave-in. He told me the names of the folks that were watching the children but they didn't live there anymore.

"I didn't know what to do. I just floated around for, oh, I don't know, it seemed like forever. And then I had this dream one night. There was this hawk sitting on a tree, and he told me to not give up hope, to keep looking. He said something about some flowers. I went to Seven Springs and asked around. I talked to the people at the mine and they told me that three had been rescued, but one had died, one was with his family, and one had been so crippled up that he was begging on the street corners.

"I was afraid to hope, but I prayed that the crippled boy was my son. Being alive, holding him close, having him with me, I wanted him any way I could get him. Letty, it *was* him. I took him to a hotel and for a long time, he didn't know who he was, and when he remembered, he didn't want anyone else to know.

"He was so ashamed of his limp and having to use a cane. He felt that he could never care for his children and that they were better off wherever they were. We talked long into the night, and then, we decided we'd find us some family.

"We went to the last address I had for the only relative I could think of, Aunt Patience, but the maid told us she died. She was a real friendly sort and she also told us about the will and what a ruckus it caused. She was really talkative. She said that Patience's niece's husband had just been sent to jail for gambling embezzled bank money. Patience left a sum of money to take care of her granddaughter since she expected something like that to happen.

"She suggested we go see a Mister Franklin McDougan. Needless to say, here we are. We had no idea that Wade's precious children were here until we talked to Mister McDougan. He didn't tell us much. He said you'd fill us in on the details. How'd that happen, Baby Sister?"

Letty laughed and cried at the same time, she sniffled and then blew her nose. Finally, she was able to talk. "I'll tell you everything, Elijah, but you're gonna have a hard time believing it. I know I did."

She started at the beginning, the day the dreams of the flowers in the fields and the hawk told her to save them. She went on about the conversation she overheard after the funeral and Mr. McDougan's help in adopting the children. She closed her eyes, blinked hard but the tears came anyway when she told of Patience leaving her the gold mine, and the news that the children were her own blood relation.

Letty rose, went to a carved box on the mantle and took out the clay medallion that Franklin had given her. "Elijah, is this yours?" She brought the medallion to the table and handed it to him.

He took it gently, and held it tenderly to his chest. "This was Isaac's, Letty. He gave it to Daniel when he was born. He wanted it passed down and somehow, I think he knew, or at least, he felt that Daniel was going to be Papa's oldest grandson. I still have mine. It's the only thing I've kept all these years."

"Aunt Letty, the turkey," Chloe cried. She frantically jumped up and ran to the stove.

"Don't burn yourself, honey, I'll get it." Letty hurried toward the oven and the spell of yesterday's memories was broken.

Letty and Chloe, with the children's help, set the table and placed all the Christmas food on the table. With Elijah at one end and Wade at the other, Letty and the children, along the Joseph, sat on the long benches on either side. Elijah said grace and had everyone in tears again by the time he'd finished.

Wade smiled and touched his children's hands as if he were afraid they'd disappear any moment.

The meal was a leisurely, social affair. Joseph talked

about Daisy and admitted they had discussed marriage and that Daisy was eager to see the children again. He said he would bring her in the summer to show her the beauty of the mountain and spend time with the children.

Shortly after the meal was put away, Joseph thanked them heartily and insisted he had to get back to town before dark. The children hugged and thanked him for bringing them their father and grandfather. He left with a letter from Letty to Franklin telling him he was always in their prayers, along with their thanks for all he had done for their family.

The children gathered around their father showing him all the gifts St. Nicholas had given them and the gifts they had made for each other.

Letty and Elijah sat by the fire talking about family members that had lived in the mountains before Elijah had left and he caught Letty up on his life in the north. The fire burned down when Eveline crept quietly over to Letty and whispered, "Aunt Letty, Papa's fallen asleep. What shall we do?"

"See if you can slip his shoes off and we'll just throw a blanket over him and let him rest. This has been a long day for the poor, dear, man. I'm sure he'll sleep through the night. We'll prepare his room tomorrow and he can get settled in.

"Elijah, you must be exhausted, too. Your old room is fixed up. Let me show you."

"Letty, I lived here seventeen years. I know where that room is. You've got to be as tired as I am, more so, with all that food you fixed. You get yourself on to bed and I'll do the same. I hope this isn't too much on you," Elijah said, frowning.

"Elijah, this is such a joy. I've never felt better. I've been alone so long, this is a blessing. I hope you don't have any plans to take off again. You and Wade are home now. There's more than enough room for all of us. We need each other, don't we?"

Her brother grabbed her hand and kissed it. "I was hoping you'd say that. There's plenty of work around here to do. We'll have this place in shape in no time. Wade needs a place to call home and things for him to do. I think he can truly recover here and get back to his old self, maybe not physically, but mentally." He hugged her and turned to his grandchildren. "Come here, young'uns, and give Grandpa a hug.

They raced to him, nearly knocking him down. Hugs and kisses were given by all. After whispering goodnight so they would not wake their father, they all tiptoed upstairs.

Letty went to her room, undressed and slipped into her nightgown. She slid under the covers, her head still swimming from the events of the day. In her prayers, she gave thanks for her all of her blessings. She blessed Aunt Patience, the children, her brother, her nephew, Joseph and Franklin. She asked the Lord to make sure that their Mama and Papa and Elijah's wife knew that Elijah was safely home, and that Wade's wife knew that Wade and their children would have a good life. She thanked her Maker for all her blessings, and her full house. And then she asked that all the hawks in the world be watched over.

The next morning when Letty opened her eyes, she lay in bed for a moment or two enjoying the wonder of her new life. Her nose twitched and she realized the aroma of coffee was drifting under her door. She quickly dressed and when she walked into the living room, she saw Wade pouring her a cup of coffee.

"I figured you're an early riser and thought you might like coffee made for you for a change." He gave her the familiar crooked grin he inherited from his father. "It's been awhile, but it tastes pretty good to me."

Letty took a sip and smiled. "It's wonderful, Wade, dear. Thank you. Did you sleep well or did that lumpy old chair make you stiff?"

"I slept better than I have in years, Aunt Letty. I can't tell you how much I appreciate you caring for my, uh, our children. I worried day and night about them. I blamed myself for going off, although all I wanted was a good job so I could give them more," he said sadly. "Then I worried that I couldn't provide at all and they would be ashamed of me for failing them and their ma."

"All's well that ends well," Letty told him. "The children are safe and have you and their grandfather back in their lives. I have a family, and you and Elijah have a future. Strange events have altered our lives and strange events have repaired them. Don't question the whys, and don't regret the past. Your father and your Uncle Isaac used to go up into the mountains and watch the hawks for hours, sometimes days. Isaac once told me he never saw a hawk cry over a missed opportunity, they only concentrated on the next. They were strong, brave, hopeful and determined, and those boys used those traits throughout their lives. It helped find you and the children.

"These mountain mornings will cure almost anything. The children will be up soon and anxious to show you around. Don't let them overtire you. You have a whole lifetime to see your new mountain home."

Before long, the kitchen was filled with laughter and love. Happy children, contented adults, and a peaceful world waited to accept a reunited mountain family.

The next several weeks passed happily. Fences were mended, the chicken coop repaired, stall boards replaced, and the barn was cleaned top to bottom. After the owl had left for a night of hunting, the children tackled the loft, sweeping, cleaning and scrubbing the rafter where the owl sat. This mountain was home to everyone, and Letty wanted it comfortable for humans and critters alike.

The snow began to melt, the icicles started to drip, and Chloe ran into the house one day holding a tiny white flower she'd found in a little patch of grass.

"Spring is just around the corner, children. The thaw has started. School will be starting in a couple of weeks as soon as the road is clear. This is a good time to have a family reunion," Letty said, smiling. She gathered everyone together and they started across the yard, through the stand of trees and up the tiny hill.

As they knelt down, pulling weeds and clipping grass and the bases of the stones, Chloe and Daniel walked around, calling out names. "Who was Samuel Mason, Aunt Letty?"

"He was your great-great uncle, my great-grandmother's brother. The woman next to him is his wife, Sudie. She was a sweet lady. Everyone here is related to you, sweetie, one way or another."

By mid-afternoon, they were finished. They sat on a blanket, telling stories about past memories. Letty laughed at Elijah as he told about jokes and pranks he and Isaac had pulled when they were children.

The mountain was peaceful and serene as if what it had been waiting for had finally arrived. In the far side of the meadow a young doe and her first fawn timidly wandered out of the woods and began grazing. Birds filled the sky and sang the joy of the coming spring. Squirrels chattered in the high branches of the trees, and the world appeared to be celebrating the coming together of the mountains' lost family. The waiting was over, and everything was complete.

Grace sat in Letty's lap, and leaned against her arm. Eli and Oliver sat on either side of Elijah, and Daniel sat by his father. Chloe and Eveline were on opposite sides of Letty, each laying their head on her shoulders.

Wade, with Daniel's help, rose to his feet and looked admiringly around the mountainside. Daniel looked up and pointed into the sky. He shaded his eyes with one and asked, "Grandpa, look, is that your hawk? Look, Grandpa, there's two of them."

The hawks circled the small clearing, peering down with shining eyes. One angled his wings and dipped down over the family while they watched. His cry echoed over the mountains, answered by his mate when she joined him.

For several minutes, Letty and her newly found family watched the graceful birds and listened to their calls. The hawks turned, gained altitude and disappeared over the forest, Letty felt a hand slip into hers. She turned and saw Elijah standing next to her with tear-filled eyes.

"I can't help but think that could be Isaac. You know, expressing his pleasure that we're all together at last. We used to spend so much time planning the day when we'd return to the mountain. I think he's glad that day finally arrived. Here we are, all together where we belong."

"And just think, Grandpa, we have all the mountain mornings in the world to start our new lives. Each day is going to be just like a fairy tale. You know how they go, once upon a time?" Grace asked.

"Yes, my darling, you're right and from now on our lives are going to be like a fairytale, except ours will begin 'Once Upon a Mountain'."

~ End ~

145